D1525544

TANCAT

A "MISS BENNETT " MYSTERY

Leighla Frances Whipper

iUniverse, Inc.
New York   Bloomington

TANCAT
A "MISS BENNETT " MYSTERY

iUniverse books may be ordered through booksellers or by contacting:

iUniverse
1663 Liberty Drive
Bloomington, IN 47403
www.iuniverse.com
1-800-Authors (1-800-288-4677)

Because of the dynamic nature of the Internet, any Web addresses or links contained in this book may have changed since publication and may no longer be valid. This is a work of fiction. All of the characters, names, incidents, organizations, and dialogue in this novel are either the products of the author's imagination or are used fictitiously.

ISBN: 978-1-4502-2530-4 (pbk)
ISBN: 978-1-4502-2531-1 (ebk)

Printed in the United States of America

iUniverse rev. date: 12/2/10

CHAPTER 1

There would, of course, be nothing in the mail that she had not, indirectly, sent to herself; subscriptions to magazines, various specialized catalogues from luxury stores, and occasional advertisements from companies who had gleaned her name from mailing lists bought from the firms she patronized. There had never been a personal letter nor did she expect any, but there could be one important exception and it had happened today. She saw the late issue of Vogue Magazine stuffed into the shining brass mailbox of her East Side New York luxury apartment building.

Miss Bennett, for that was now her name, extracted it after removing her fur-lined gloves with freshly manicured fingers. It was February, and the aftermath of a heavy blizzard had made her winter outfit mandatory. The full-length dark mink coat with matching fur hat and lined suede boots made her a possible candidate to pose for the cover of the magazine she now held. Gathering up the three small boxes of her shopping, she made her way to the private elevator to her apartment.

The anonymous twentieth floor at last. Her penthouse with its private foyer and entrance was quite apart and she liked to think of herself on a desert island, but of course an island in the center of a teeming city and with all the amenities. As she entered, she again appreciated the welcoming comfort, which reflected everything that years of good taste, wide travel and wise auction purchases had wrought.

First had come the soundproofing, so necessary when she wanted concert level on her stereo unit. It also gave more privacy when she practiced on the Bosendorfer grand she had located with much difficulty. The focus of the exquisite room with its mushroom-toned walls and furniture was geared to the large terrace whose wide sheet-glass doors gave on to the view of the East River. They now framed the falling snow against a pale gray background of fog -- all in sharp contrast to the comfortable interior.

The cat, Emily, jumped from her down pillow on one of the couches and ran to her. Emily, to some, might have struck the only jarring note, for she somehow did not match her surroundings. Neither an arrogant Siamese nor a fluffy Persian, she could only be classified as a domestic tabby with her short gray and white fur containing darker markings. As a kitten, she had been within minutes of being collected by the Humane Society truck. Only its delay in traffic had saved her. The doorman had complained to Miss Bennett who happened to be on her way in at that moment that he could not understand why every stray animal always seemed to arrive at the door of his building and tended to hang around him. He added that he now knew the number of the Humane Society from memory.

What impulse had made her take the half-sick kitten with the gummy eyes, obviously needing nourishment and a veterinarian, she never knew? But Emily -- so named by the doorman himself, after two weeks of adjustment, seemed to have been with her always. She had grown into contented and intelligent cat hood, raised on the choicest of cat and people food. Today she knew there was something special, signaled by the rattling of the outside wrapping of a small silver-papered container, which she eagerly watched being extracted.

"Something you'll like," she announced to the purring animal arching around her ankles. "Crabmeat straight from the Chesapeake Bay."

Emily made grateful noises and led the way into the tiled kitchen where her special plate was waiting. Miss Bennett threw off her heavy coat before following, revealing a figure which spoke more of twenty-five years than the thirty-three she was. The beige wool from the Cardin boutique helped, of course.

She marveled, not for the first time, how Emily always ate as though she had been starved for days. Returning to the living room, she adjusted her short dark coiffure, sank into the pillows of a couch and took up the magazine with a stirring interest. She had another assignment.

Slowly she turned the pages, noting the various European collections, making mental notes of the styles that might interest her. She lingered over several pages of accessories before coming on the message she knew would be on page one hundred. At the top in block letters she read:

KENNEDY AIRPORT

FEBRUARY

27

9:00

A.M.

AEREONAVES

AIRLINES

DEPARTURE

BUILDING

MEXICO CITY

The group usually met in a modest restaurant on Barrow Street. Word was passed with two or three phone calls. The meetings were only semi-social for the hard core of business could never have been transacted in a public place. That sort of meeting was held less often and at an almost hidden rendezvous in upstate New York with others. The Gold Coin suited them very well -- up to now perfectly. The food was excellent, prepared by the French owner-chef from Provence. The single pianist did not play rock and roll, but featured an undemanding repertoire of Vernon Duke, Cole Porter and Gershwin songs which served not only as a pleasant background for dining, but also as a natural cover for the almost elliptical conversation of the group. Also he did not sing -- a fact appreciated by most of the customers. Then too the bartender was ideal. They had often commented on this as he was not one of the talkative school with the obvious and unnecessary tricks to charm bigger tips from the clientele. He knew his job and stuck to it.

One could not get a better martini or Rob Roy anywhere. Still he was not one of those smart-alecs -- a know-it- all ready to instruct anyone. Whatever one wanted, one got with a polite smile, and he remembered everyone's preference no matter how long the absence.

The Gold Coin was indeed ideal -- not too large or too small, no news people clientele and no crazy kids nor arrogant executives and certainly no "society." Those frequented the "boites" and bistros and clubs on the East Side. Best of all it had not been written up in the food columns of the leading New York newspaper, for that would have spoiled everything for them. They had had to change twice before on that account. Too many people had flocked in and therefore their strict prerequisites had been lost. To the casual observer they might have been five average businessmen having a few drinks and staying on to dinner before getting home on a late commuter train. Their suits ran mostly to Oxford gray flannel or a muted check with correctly blending or contrasting accessories.

As Don regarded them, he weighed, not for the first time, the possibility of staying on the job longer instead of quitting as he had often promised himself, to devote himself entirely to his doctorate thesis at Columbia University. He was a psychology major. Yet the salary and tips were so good here at the Gold Coin that the temptation to stay on was great, especially since he had several friends with degrees who had been long unemployed.

At the moment, his roving eye took in the picture of what was his favorite party. Two fathers and two sons plus another all engaged in what he suspected was a going business or businesses outside of state and federal laws. His professional analysis took into account the good tailors who undoubtedly selected their ties, shirts and shoes, for the accents of the older men bespoke not only a foreign country, but somehow up from peasantry. The sons were seemingly polished, displaying respect for their elders and a certain protective manner toward them. However, the group was undoubtedly cohesive, an in-group with their own private language and rules.

Their tipping was always normal -- good but normal. Their cars, he had found, did not run to imports or the top American products. There were the standards -- nor did they seem to change models yearly. Just good middle-class mores and customs, he summed up, but all within their own special pattern.

These reflections did not interfere with his efficient shaking of a Hennessy stinger for another table now finishing dessert, nor did anything change the concentration on his almost handsome face. He casually poured the mixture into the correct chilled glasses and flicked his eyes over the various tables checking for possible wine re-orders, not trusting the two well-meaning but inefficient waiters to see to it.

There was a genuine bonhommerie at their table tonight. They had not seen each other for almost a month and things had gone reasonably well, not only for them personally, but also for their joint enterprises during that period. George let it be known that the government at last seemed to be letting him alone over the matter of his income tax. A battery of his accountants had been in conference many times with what he called the "Feds." He now had enough legitimate businesses to be able to declare a pretty good amount -- enough to satisfy authorities. He announced that he was a businessman above reproach as did the others who backed him and almost in chorus affirmed that they too were substantial elements of their communities, giving generous donations to the various fund drives, always having their houses and lawns well-kept for the neighborhood pride, never taking advantage of any of the petty rules and regulations involved with city and suburban living, gladly recycling their trash, in short adhering to every requisite of being a good citizen -- an ideal citizen.

"It takes a lot of patience to earn an honest dollar," George concluded sententiously. "What about you, Henry? They still on your neck too?"

"They ain't never got off'n it," Henry replied not failing to note the visible flinching of his son across the table. He realized he had made some grammatical error. That was the trouble sending the offspring to college. They got to know too damn much and lorded it over their parents. But he couldn't say the boy wasn't clever. He always handled his end of their various projects entrusted to him very well indeed.

"Dad's all straight with everything," Anthony added to his father's statement. "We went through all that tax examination too. But we've been careful." He gave his winning smile around -- a smile touched with a bit of gloating in the eyes. "We outlasted them."

A friendly silence reigned. They were shortly served the main course on which Armand had excelled. The chef always extended extra effort for them, having discovered that he was appreciated. In a small place, one could anticipate preferences and it was a fine thing to know that one's efforts were not wasted. Also, in this case neither was one's excellent wine cellar. No rough red wine for them. One of the younger ones did the wine ordering and Armand approved his selections. He now stole a look at the table from the small glass panel on his green baize-swinging door. Fine. They were beginning to eat with gusto -- but yet not too fast.

"Well, what's new with our little joint project," Victor asked, turning to Anthony who confidently smiled.

"Another client recently," he answered with pride. It was always a pleasure to have good news for Victor who could be called the leader of the table. It was good to prove that he could handle a delicate task well for all to see. "I channeled it to that woman. She's never failed us yet. It's someplace in Mexico -- near Mexico City. The job's political -- meaning it pays well."

"That's the damnedest thing," George commented. "I would never in the wide world have picked a woman for that kind of work."

"Never failed yet!" Anthony repeated. "Remember I spotted her at the pistol range at the Athletic Club. She's got dead aim. Then when I had her followed out to the rifle range, they said she was phenomenal!"

An appreciative silence ensued before he continued. "A real oddball if I ever saw one. Keeps herself to herself. Naturally, I had her shadowed a while before contact."

"Best kind for this work," Victor murmured.

"As a matter of fact, we've never met -- did I tell you? All contact is written. More protection for us- It's only _her_ neck. I arranged to leave the emolument in her apartment. And while she's out!"

"What the heck's an emolument?" Victor growled. "Talk English."

Anthony laughed even though nettled. "Her loot, her bread, her compensation if you prefer."

They joined him in laughter as he continued. "Ideal situation. Wish we could arrange the same for the others. The less you know -- well, the less you know!"

"Amen!" came from several voices.

"I'll drink to that." Victor said reaching for his glass.

Suddenly Don appeared holding a cobwebby bottle of Richebourg Roman Conte. He was sure the cobwebs would impress the younger two and made a small production of removing them. Although clad in his impeccable white mess jacket and black trousers, his manner was as gracious as though he wore the sommelier's chain, and equally authoritative.

"Ah, perfect," young John exclaimed. For it was now his turn. If Anthony thought he was so smart with his careful and expert ordering of the meal, showing off his good French, he, Johnny, could hold his own when it came to wine. He knew too that his father would want him to show up well in some department of culture for he too had been sent to a good college. He and Don went through the ritual of the tasting after the careful opening of the bottle. Then savoring the sip and wisely nodding, the signal was given that it met with approval. He made a clever toast, previously thought out, and geared to the older men's frame of reference, thus warming his father's heart.

It was a festive evening what with their regular businesses and concessions all running well, their various encounters with the law ironed out, their joint sidelines with Anthony in charge flourishing, and no current feuds or vendettas to see to. Established territories were still adhered to, and now there was a tacit agreement to enjoy, enjoy. No need to look too far into the future. The moment was now.

CHAPTER 2

Emily was aware they were going to take a trip. The cat always knew when Miss Bennett began packing and she made short excursions around the bedroom, into the open door of the walk-in closet, back into the living room and finished by jumping on the bed sniffing at the faint perfume of the clothes carefully folded, ready to be placed into the luggage. She loved these changes and had grown accustomed to her carrying case, which was always carefully placed under the forward seat. Miss Bennett, as she worked, was thinking of the climates she would encounter not only in cool Mexico City, but also in Cuernavaca which she knew was subtropical. It was hard to avoid stepping on Emily who now in her excitement seemed intent upon charging across her path as she moved around the room.

In little more than an hour, all was ready. Miss Bennett slowed her pace and occasionally sat staring into space. Her eyes, usually gray, lost focus in the soft lighting and seemed to take on a neutral color. She moved from the bed, Emily following, and sat on the lounge in front of the living room fireplace, watching the flames. Half an hour passed with Emily settled beside her. Almost hypnotized by the flickering she felt her mind go blank as an old familiar feeling began to take over.

Suddenly she jumped up, badly frightening Emily. Confusedly she ran to her closet, snatched her coat and hurriedly began putting on her boots. With only a silk scarf over her head she rushed from the apartment to order her car.

Within twenty minutes she was speeding uptown toward the George Washington Bridge where she would take the turn off to Englewood. The leftover packed-down slick snow from previous storms slowed the car as she left the bridge, and she skidded several times before drawing up into the driveway of a modest one-story house. She entered quickly with her key, turned on the light in the small living room and breathed a sigh of relief from the tension of dealing with the heavy evening traffic after a snowstorm.

She partially raised one of the frilly curtained windows and let the fresh air blow in. Looking around she saw it was exactly the same. Nothing had changed. The old upright piano was still in the corner, sheet music turned to the same song. On top were the folios containing the Bach fugues. She walked through, inspected the bedroom and the small dinette giving off the smaller kitchen. Throwing off her coat and scarf, she changed her boots for an old pair of shoes she fished from a closet and reached for her apron, which hung behind the kitchen door.

"I must hurry," she murmured, "she'll be home any minute now and there's nothing cooked."

The freezer of the refrigerator yielded a chicken and various packages of vegetables which she immediately set about to defrost and prepare. She worked efficiently, occasionally talking to herself. "I still have time," she whispered, "I'm sure she stopped at the library. Otherwise she would be home from school by now. Good

I always leave the thermostat on low. Otherwise there's never time to heat the place adequately before she gets here."

She now raised the temperature needle, thinking she wanted no more problems, as Terry's lungs were really never very strong. She turned on the small table radio and enjoyed some of her popular favorites.

Time passed quickly and now there was something more deliberate in her movements, which gradually became uncoordinated. But she went through with the work of getting the chicken into the oven and the vegetables in saucepans.

Five detached houses to the right on the same street, the Everett family had gathered for dinner. In spite of the uncertainties of the commuter trains, Mr. Everett insisted that they eat at least one meal together daily, and because of the different schedules of his son, daughter and his wife, that meal of course had to be dinner. Both youngsters studied at a nearby college and easily arranged their studies to coincide with the dinner hour. The part-time accounting Mrs. Everett did for a nearby firm permitted her to complete all her house chores now that the children were out of the way, walk the short distance to her job, return to shop in stores on the way home and have dinner on the table with no problems. She prided herself on this handling of two separate careers and occasionally boasted of it at her monthly bridge club Saturday meetings.

Tonight she had taken the time to roast a leg of lamb, adorned with browned new potatoes. Also present was the mint jelly along with asparagus and a Caesar salad.

"There's dessert," she smiled, "so save room for it."

"This is super, Mom," Ben pronounced eyeing the table. "Outdid yourself I do believe, and it's not even Sunday!"

"And since I helped put it on the table, you can help me clear up afterwards," his sister, Dorothy, quickly cut in. "You always get out of doing anything around the house."

"For the love of Pete -- we've got a dishwasher. Nobody has to wash dishes," he retorted.

"That's what you always say," she began, "but somebody has to clear the table and..."

"OK you two," their father interrupted, "I get enough bickering at the office every day without you two starting up at home every night!"

"Let's just eat before it all gets cold," warned his wife, by now quite used to the often repeated scene.

The telephone rang sharply at this moment to the dismay of everyone.

"Make it short whoever it is," directed Mrs. Everett as Dorothy went to answer.

"They should know anyone would be eating dinner around this time," her husband grumbled as he began carving.

In a few moments, Dorothy returned considerably upset.

"<u>Her?</u>" they chorused raggedly, making a question of it. But they knew exactly what she meant. A silence fell as Dorothy resumed her place at the table.

"Yes, the same old questions -- Did you and Terry stop at the library? Where could she be? Dinner's ready and she hasn't come home."

"She's crazy after all this time," Mr. Everett said resuming his carving.

Mrs. Everett seemed to go to pieces, trembling as she reached for the gravy boat. "It's been three years -- three long years since it happened! Why can't she forget?"

"Raped and murdered -- Terry shouldn't have taken that shortcut." Ben said gratuitously, earning exasperated glances from the others.

"She's sick. She should be in a sanitarium," Mrs. Everett mused. "I thought she wouldn't bother us any more. And to think, Dorothy, you almost always followed Terry's lead; it could have happened to you too..."

"Mom! We agreed we'd never never talk about that anymore!" Dorothy protested.

"That's right," Ben chimed in, "We agreed..."

"Oh, shut up!" Mr. Everett broke in angrily, knowing that now the entire evening was ruined, as well as the dinner. None of them now had appetite. They would go through the motions.

But Mrs. Everett, in a world of her own, was not paying attention. "And to think he's never been caught. Murder by person or persons unknown..." she trailed off.

The chicken had been ready for some time, and she was only waiting to put the biscuits in at the last minute. The house was good and warm now; the table was set and the radio now tuned to the station playing only classical selections. Her thoughts turned now to her husband. Ironic that he had not lived to see how his daughter had developed -- she was first in her high school class and had earned the scholarship to the New England college offered to the Valedictorian of the graduating class, fulfilling her early promise. But now why didn't she call -- why so late? She began to hurry almost rushing, turning the oven off, putting the chicken in the warmer, lowering the flame under the saucepans. But it was useless. For some time she had remembered who she now was and why she was there. The futility overwhelmed her as she extinguished all the burners, turned off the radio and flung herself on the living room couch sobbing. She lay there for hours until falling into an exhausted sleep lasting until dawn.

She caught her plane the next day with only moments to spare. A mandatory special visit to Mr. Gerard, her hairdresser, had delayed her. The ticket was waiting for her at the counter along with an envelope which she knew would contain the minimum of instructions. It had always been this way. Nobody to account to, only the briefest contact with a cover if one was necessary -- a person she would never again meet. All now cut and dried -- only the maximum demand -- success. She must complete her assignment, and the expectation was mutually understood between employer and employee -- a silent understanding. Dead aim was her profession and her pride, working with her small jeweled thirty-two imagining the face of that unknown man before her when she fired. How satisfying to pull the trigger and to kill Terry's murderer and violator over and over. To pretend it was the killer each time.

The stewardess took her beige sheared beaver jacket to hang in an alcove. Returning, she helped her put Emily who was being good inside her cage, under the seat in front. Then bringing her a special Bloody Mary, she left with the thought that the slight puffiness she had noted in her face was probably the result of a farewell party the night before, for this passenger, she was sure, was one of the beautiful people who jetted at her whim anywhere in the world. She surmised that the beaver was surely imported from Denmark and cost quite a few big ones if a penny. The thin red wool under it she recognized as couturier -- Paris or Italy -- hard to tell these days. She reflected that some people had all the luck and when was she ever going to be in that number? Three years of flying a choice route and no millionaire had yet proposed marriage. Proposals, yes, but marriage, no.

Arriving at Juarez International Airport in Mexico City was like leaving the black and white picture of New York with its brown-black slush of past and present snowstorms and stepping into Technicolor. The balmy air, polluted, perhaps, but still balmy encouraged the passengers to shed their winter coats even as they passed Immigration and Customs. The sun was shining and most of the officials were smiling.

She emerged into the waiting room and after only a moment's pause, was approached by a black-suited, middle-aged Mexican who told her in somewhat broken English that he was Pepe Valente, her chauffeur, at her service and would she please follow him to the waiting car. He directed the porter who had taken charge of her luggage and added that they would drive to her villa in Cuernavaca about an hour or so from the capital.

There was little point in asking how he had identified her, as everything had followed the same pattern of the past. He would only tell her that the villa in Cuernavaca had been rented by mail, and that he had received a long-distance call that morning describing her features and what she would be wearing. She was uncaring, but always aware that persons invisible to her, unknown to her were employing her, making the arrangements, overseeing her, directing her by cryptic messages and later, after the job, paying her anonymously. The money was invariably to be found in crisp small bills filling four pockets of two bathrobes hanging in one of her bedroom closets.

She knew that within a day or two, she would be contacted in some way by a person who would use the operative word,

"Tancat." She had been so advised by the brief note inside her ticket envelope, which she had read on the plane.

The ride was over a winding flower-bedecked highway with its endless curves through mountains and around mountains, descending into even more radiant warmth. As she sat in the back of the Mercedes and listened to Pepe's history of the villa she would occupy, she listened with only half an ear. Appreciative of the change from the New York storms, her only serious thought at the moment was the location of a good hairdresser and the possibility of buying a stock of the hand-embroidered cotton dresses she had seen on previous trips to the area.

"My wife and I will always be at your service," Pepe was saying. "I'm the caretaker and chauffeur, my wife, Maria, is the cook and we have a cleaning maid, Yolanda." He added that they were often bored with nobody to look after since the owners spent more of their time in Europe. The man was an ex-politician who found it convenient to absent himself for several years from the country. Rambling on, Pepe mentioned that he was sure the gardens and grounds would be the ideal place for her to rest after a strenuous social season. Thus she gathered that she was to play the role of the jaded socialite.

As his English became more unintelligible, she suggested that they employ Spanish. Immediately Pepe brightened and quite immune to the danger of a hairpin curve approaching, he turned around gratefully to say, "This is very good. My wife and Yolanda speak no English at all, so now we can all understand each other with the language of God -- Castellano -- Spanish!"

She nodded in agreement as he turned in the nick of time to avoid running off an unguarded precipice. Later when arrival was imminent they passed more slowly through the drowsing streets with their high flower-laden walls shielding stucco houses.

The villa was imposing. Maria, Pepe's wife, stood in front of the wide-open carved iron doors of the driveway to greet them. She was attended by the young maid. Afterward Pepe dealt with her considerable luggage while Maria accompanied her inside for a cursory tour of the house. There was a two-story living room in authentic Spanish colonial style with an enormous winding carved wood staircase leading to the surrounding balcony. Cool and perfect in its checkered sunlight, the place spoke of centuries of tradition. The polished ebony parquet floor was covered with priceless Oriental rugs; window frames of carved wood encased the beveled glass of the mullioned windows now open showing a large garden filled with rose bushes and creeping bougainvillea along the high walls; the alcove with its grand piano and harp, she noted with pleasure, as well as the heavily framed oil paintings which she was sure were authentic Yelazquez.

"This house dates from the Spanish conquest, "Pepe explained seeing her appreciation. "It has had only three families as owners, but several generations of the same families. The present owner is in Spain, but I doubt he'll come back any time soon. He might want to sell -- this was never his taste. He only owned it for four years." His tone told her he did not approve of the man.

"It was rented by mail, the agent said," he continued. "I have worked here all my life -- born here in the gate house. My grandfather and father worked here too. In those days we had lots of help -- two gardeners, horses in the stables, cook with assistants, maids -- everything we needed. We were really a hacienda, growing our own food and flowers for the house, making our own bread, growing feed for the animals -- horses, cows and even goats -- and now look -- most of the land sold off. Only the house and gardens left..." He trailed off disconsolately.

"But there seems to still be a lot of land left," she reminded him as she picked up Emily's cage. "The house is simply lovely. Just the kind of place I can enjoy -- quiet -- cool -- restful."

Pepe brightened at this and took over the opening of the cage, exclaiming as the cat jumped out, paused to get Oriented, and began to wash herself vigorously.

"A nice cat," he commented. "It seems to travel all right."

"She's used to it," she replied turning to the stairs where the maid was waiting to show her to her bedroom.

Upstairs was also in the colonial style with the patina of years of good care shining on the hand-wrought wood. Two heavy glass doors opened from her bedroom to a balcony riotous with purple vines. The afternoon February sun was gentle and birds were chattering in the garden below.

"Dinner will be ready in an hour, if you wish," Yolanda shyly told her, smoothing an imaginary wrinkle on the hand-crocheted bedspread whose posters reached almost to the ceiling. She then began unpacking and to Miss Bennett's surprise, professionally hanging dresses or refolding lingerie before laying it in the drawers of the large bureau and the armoire.

Emily had followed them upstairs and continued to shake her fur while looking around as if adjusting and settling her nerves.

After changing into cooler brown linen, Miss Bennett, followed by Emily went outside to walk around the inviting grounds. The peace was welcome as was the beauty of the quiet walks edged with foliage and brilliantly colored flowers, hedges and trees. A blended fragrance, including gardenia, hung on the air. Emily ran after low-flying butterflies, and investigated the shrubbery, sniffing with the careful curiosity of a city-bred apartment cat.

Turning a corner of one of the narrow pebbled walks, the two stopped in amazement as a dream swimming pool stretched out before them. It was large and irregularly shaped in the form of petals of an enormous flower. Ringed by flowering azalea bushes, it harbored every convenience a swimmer could wish for. High and low diving boards met the eye as did lounge chairs, some with tables. Half hidden by magnolia trees at one end were vine-covered structures, which were obviously dressing rooms. Crystalline waters revealed Italian tiles arranged in underwater murals depicting Neptune surrounded by his court.

Except for the occasional passing breeze gently rippling the water and the humming of unseen insects, the scene could have been a painting. She wondered if she were dreaming the entire panorama -- the still life. Even Emily abandoned her sorties and sniffed at the difference in the fresher air, still using great caution. Venturing into one of the dressing rooms Miss Bennett found swimsuits in various sizes. A glance at her watch told her they still had half an hour before dinner, so she quickly changed into a blue suit found to be her size and within minutes she was swimming the petal design of the pool, ringing it, observed by Emily from a safe distance on the edge. In the depths of the tepid water, New York and snow seemed eons away. What had happened the night before was gently fading into the background of the present. It was hard now to remember. She was here, and as usual in the lap of luxury with a job to do.

Twenty minutes refreshed her. Later, composed and dressed with her wet hair bound by a chiffon scarf, she sat down at the head of what seemed an endless dining room table to be served by Maria and Yolanda. Emily was served a can of her favorite food brought from New York, and she ate heartily, nerves or no nerves.

Night fell quickly after an incredibly beautiful but short sunset which had painted the sky rose and gold, forming the background for the distant volcano. Miss Bennett went upstairs into her bedroom and slowly unmade her bed, folding and stacking the heavy embroidered linen sheets on a chair and remaking it with her preferred flowered percale sheets she traveled with, glad that these and her special blankets were large enough to cover the entire colonial size of the bed. Her small radio on the night table played several of her favorite Mexican songs by Agustin Lara and Guty Cardenas. She then placed Emily's bed in a corner and settled herself in the large, well-padded armchair to read again the communication that had been left for her at the airline desk at Kennedy.

The note was brief, as all of them had been in the past. Her instructions were simple as usual, containing one name and a telephone number. The name, she knew, was that of her next victim and the number was that of a New York public telephone -- always different for each job -- to be called only in an emergency and only between certain definite hours of the day. It would, she knew, be that of a pay phone on one of the busier sections of downtown New York. It would be covered during the given hours.

Unbelievingly, she read and re-read the name given and her heart accelerated.

Hitherto, her named victim had simply been anonymous, and later an anonymous face. She had done her work entirely oblivious to any motive behind the assignment or the identity of those who hired her. But now, she stared almost hypnotically at the name on the page. Paco Silva. Two of his paintings hung in her New York apartment. They had been bought at tremendous prices after spirited bidding at a leading international auction house.

Slightly bewildered, she rose to slip on her nightgown -- something she had made into a ritual. Among the many she had bought on a recent visit to Paris, she selected a creation with a deep band of lace tatting around the low neckline, which supported yards of gathered white chiffon printed with tiny violets. She pushed the name of Paco Silva away as she deliberately brought to her mind the difficulty of locating someone to do the lace tatting which now really seemed to be a lost art. She then selected a book from the group she had brought with her -- something frivolous -- escape. With a spy mystery, she crept beneath her sheets, firmly rejecting any intruding thought -- an art in which she had become adept -- and immersed herself into spies in white or black trench coats working usually in heavy fogs in European cities.

The day, combined with the events of the night before, had been a taxing one. A half hour's reading was enough to invite a peaceful slumber. With only a small night light burning, she let the occasional outside night sounds lure her into forgetfulness. A gentle wind stirred the sighing trees near her balcony. Some night birds called softly to each other. A low humming of the garden insects all merged to create a concerto -- a prelude to pleasant dreams she occasionally experienced. It could be one of those good nights, she thought as she sank into her down pillows and closed her eyes.

She awoke with a start. The digital clock told her it was three in the morning. But she knew she had heard something in her sleep, something alien to the nature sounds without. She kept perfectly still until she heard it again. Sure of it now, she knew it came from downstairs and had drifted up through the well of the two-story living room, which acted as a perfect sound conduit to her bedroom off the interior balcony. She stealthily sat up, remembering that Pepe and his family lived in the gatehouse outside.

With the same care, she rose, pulled on her robe, patting the right-hand pocket to reassure herself it was there -- her small, almost toy-like twenty-two, especially assembled for her in Italy and studded with sapphires. A toy, both deadly and aesthetic. It now gave her the familiar pleasure of a faithful companion so necessary to her present life.

Barefoot, she crept from her room to look below between the balustrades of the balcony stairway. By the light of a waning moon drifting in the windows, she saw a figure moving downstairs. The silhouette was that of a man of more than average height slowly making his way around the room. She watched closely, suspecting a burglar, but still keeping an open mind. It could be Pepe making rounds. Slowly the moments seemed to pass and she saw him apparently give up searching and begin his approach to the staircase. She noted his care to ascend silently, testing each step for creaks in the old polished wood. This took some time and gave her the chance to evaluate her position. She slipped the twenty-two back into her pocket and crouched to the side of the thick ornamental post of the top step. An eternity seemed to pass before he reached the top step about three feet from where she hid. He stood hesitating, and in that second she straightened and with practiced force she gave him a chop between chest and stomach that immediately toppled him backwards down the staircase.

She pursued him, running down, and reached the bottom a second later than her quarry. As he began to scramble to his feet, she pinned him in an arm lock which held but for a moment. He broke it so professionally that she immediately recognized the work of a karate black belt. He pushed her roughly back and was away through the open door of the patio through which he had obviously entered.

She caught her breath as she decided not to follow, knowing it to be useless. She turned on a lamp, went to the recessed bar and poured an ounce of Scotch into a glass. Seated on the bar stool, she slowly sipped it as Emily tentatively descended the steps to sit at her feet.

"Now you come!!" she scolded. "Where were you when I needed you the most?"

Emily purred and rubbed against her ankles having perfectly understood the gist of these words by the tone.

She rose late the next morning, dressed in a sleeveless blue cotton print and descended to her requested continental breakfast. Upon her questioning, the three servants assured her that all doors and windows were always carefully locked according to long custom and tradition. The night air, she was told, was not good for the delicate wood of the piano or the oil pictures. Only the dry daytime air was permitted inside, and during the rainy season the fireplace was always in use and the doors shut and usually locked by day also.

As Pepe and Maria enlarged upon this theme it developed into a tirade against the changing times of the country, the increase of crime, even in Cuernavaca. Meanwhile Miss Bennett casually examined the simple locks of the French door, noting that a child could have negotiated them. It would have been nothing for a professional. But this was different. A neat portion of one of the glass panes had been removed, perhaps simply to avoid any noise, and a hand had without the slightest trouble unlocked the door from the inside.

"Don't worry," she consoled them, "there's still no need for you to sleep in the house here. He won't return. I scared him, I'm sure."

"But nothing has been touched," Maria repeated. "I counted all the silver -- including the tea sets and trays and the antiques -- everything is as it was -- not even moved. A rare burglar for sure."

This thought had occurred earlier to Miss Bennett but she put it aside for later examination. If there were wider ramifications of her job, she preferred not to know them, yet. A man who entered stealthily by night without even trying to take any valuables though he had had every opportunity presaged a deeper set of factors, unless, of course, he were some sort of maniac determined to attack or kill any strange woman because he had somehow hated his mother as a child. She recalled his slow examination of the downstairs room as though he were searching for something definite. The height and bulk of his body and the imperfect glimpse of his face in the moonlight before she struck him all suggested an Anglo-Saxon' though she knew she could easily be wrong on this point. She had known several legitimately blond Mexicans, Spaniards and Italians, most of whom had been tall and broad-shouldered.

Although she tried again to put the incident from her mind, she was aware of something forgotten, something experienced in the encounter which now eluded her because of the violence involved.

And now she asked herself where is there a good manicurist and hairdresser? And where were those hand-embroidered cottons to be found? The job could take weeks, and she would probably need more cotton things than she had brought. Later Pepe drove her to the various small stores featuring typical Mexican

25

specialties. Nearby she also located an excellent beauty salon where she spent the entire morning, reserving the early afternoon for shopping' She now felt herself drifting into her usual routine, kept in any place she found herself.

"We are happy to have the grand maestro in our midst," Pepe commented on the way back to the villa.

"The grand maestro?" she repeated, already knowing the answer, for he had made three syllables of the word, which indicated in Mexico a person of consequence -- a professional. Two syllables of the same word meant an artisan, perhaps a carpenter or a plumber.

"Yes, Maestro Francisco Silva Ibarro -- known to us as Paco Silva," he triumphantly replied. "I am sure you know one of the nicknames for Francisco is Paco -- also Pancho -- also Curro, but he uses Paco -- surprising in a Spaniard I think. And of course Ibarra is the name of his mother, which we Latins use after our father's name. He is here living permanently with us. Of all the countries he could have chosen to live in, he chose Mexico. And of all the beautiful cities we have in our country, he chose Cuernavaca, the City of Eternal Spring! Imagine!"

"Yes, how flattering," she replied.

"He lives very near our home," Pepe enthused. I can drive past his villa. Of course there is not much one can see with the high walls, but we can drive by anyway -- all right?

"Yes, I would like to see his house. I like his work," she replied appreciating her own understatement. "As a matter of fact I have bought two of his paintings."

Pepe's face lit up. He turned to her and smiled. She realized, that she had been elevated in his estimation. She was not only the "rich socialite" but an educated, cultured, rich socialite. He turned to his driving just in time to avoid hitting a careless dog sauntering in front of the car.

Paco Silva was about to allow himself to be happy. It took some doing for he often criticized fate as it pertained to him, and expected the maximum of that entity and of the people surrounding him. But today he decided to count his blessings realizing that he should occasionally detach himself and savor his present situation, including his fame, his household, his group, and his work in progress. A summing up. Not for the first time bemused that a king had nothing more than he possessed. They were only figureheads whereas he -- Paco Silva -- had genius -- a name to go down the centuries with the world's best and most famous. Hadn't his face decorated the postage stamps of France on the eve of his sixtieth birthday? Of course this was before he had thought it wise to leave his Riviera estate and settle in Mexico. After his most vocal criticism of the government and particularly the president, there had been some pointed hints -- subtle but coming from powerful sources -- that perhaps another country would be more to his liking. The trouble with his situation was that his fame put him too much in the spotlight. Anything he said, any announcement muttered within the hearing of even a minor journalist made news. And news, which stepped on important toes.

The day was paradise. His studio with its three-story ceiling was perfect in size, lighting and ambiance. The work on hand was going reasonably well. Paco, a short rotund figure at sixty-five filled any space with his dynamic presence. His hair had departed gracefully and what was left around the sides and back had now gone white. But his face still had the strong lines and set of the Spanish man of the soil without as many of the usual wrinkles, as he had worked for decades in the shaded ateliers and studios of Paris, and later on the Riviera.

Though the Mexican sun was now burning him bronze, his skin was smooth and with this more romantic tone, he felt he looked younger. How well had he preserved himself, he ruminated, and how well had he arranged his life. His genius had been recognized before he was too old to enjoy the fruits of fame. He reflected that most of his contemporaries had passed on, some receiving fame almost immediately after death. But he, Paco, was a living legend.

What a pleasure it was to know that outside the door of his studio awaited Michele and Jeanne, both young, attractive and vying for his attention. In the twenties there had been Trini and Francesca. The thirties had yielded the ineffable Marline and the lovely Rita, and so on. How strange they all had come into his life in pairs. And how nice and really obliging he had been to paint them all, and by so doing, had immortalized them. Also the paintings seemed to have kept a sort of dairy of his life and changing painting styles.

He now eyed the broad canvas, which he hoped to finish soon. It was going well. Not even that recent attack on him in the French press had affected his work. He remembered the time when a similar article would have blocked his painting for weeks. He realized, of course, that his political views were not out of sync with those of several countries. They really did not appreciate his political philosophy and it would serve them right if he just dropped politics and concentrated on his own work.

The problem he faced was that he had begun his political life as a dedicated Communist -- a highly visible and vocal Communist appearing on the cover of international political magazines, praised or vilified depending upon the slant and politics of that magazine. He had basked in the attention of the press and took the stand that every artist owed something more than his art to the world. He invited interviews where he expounded this theory. But now that Communism had been discarded in Russia and in other countries of the world, he found himself too stubborn to renounce the view of a lifetime. So he took recourse in criticizing every country that had renounced Communism, a fact that did nothing for his popularity in those places, none of which was aware that his concept of Communism was that of a child. It was the word he was in love with and had been most of his life. Living the life of a capitalist, he rarely thought of the irony of his theoretical political beliefs, but honestly believed he was sincere. He vowed that one day he would write a book dealing with his involvement with Communism and giving his opinion of every country that had renounced. He even threatened to visit Russia to give impetus to the remnants of the party now almost powerless in the congress of Yeltsin. He only waited an invitation, and was sure only this remained to bolster this aspect of his reputation. Some time in the far, far distance if he ever died -- God forbid -- but just in case he ever did, the mausoleum could be inscribed -- Artist of the World -- Communist Mentor of the World.

He rearranged the order of these words several times as he glanced from the open window giving on to the large garden. His mind left the contemplation of the inscription on his tomb and bounced back to the present. I can live perhaps thirty years more in this climate, he thought, and it reminds me so much of my beloved Spain -- Andalucia. If I had stayed in that uncertain climate of Paris I'd be dead by now. He shuddered, not liking to think more about his death -- how could the world manage without a Pepe Silva? Personally he abhorred the very thought of nothingness, no women -- no work to be done, only a lonely tomb where even though well inscribed, only a few people came now and then to leave flowers. All the good things of this life passed on to others.

At this point he made a note to remind Pierre Duval, his friend and fellow painter, to hurry that wife of his along with the biography he had authorized. At first he had wanted her to emphasize only his political philosophy, but he had to think it out more fully. Meanwhile, as time was passing so fast, he had decided that she was the very person to do a more personal work which would effectively neutralize the allegations his ex-mistress, Carla, had made in her book about him. The book had left its mark, had hit a nerve. She had managed to take him off his pinnacle and bring him down among the mortals. She had mentioned his age, his stinginess, and worst of all had quoted that damned Braquelle, a colleague respected by all, who had quipped, "If Silva could only paint, he'd be damned good company!" He knew she hadn't dared to lie about this, for Braquelle was still living and in good health. Damn that bitch! Was there any justice in this world, any fairness? She had partially destroyed the image he had been perfecting all these years. Hadn't he given her a decent settlement when they had parted? How was he to know she would write that book -- or could write it? She must have had a ghostwriter, but the effect was the same!

He dropped his brush and decided to have coffee. After all, this had happened three years ago. There was no need to worry about anything. His pictures were, of course, selling extremely well, and he had long been a millionaire.

He opened the door leading to the garden and was immediately surrounded. Not only was there Michele, with her blond and highly paintable fragility, but all the cohorts had come today. As he flopped into the wide garden chair, he decided that he would make them suffer a bit in retaliation for the moment of depression he had just conquered, so he remained silent for a moment or two. This restrained them only slightly for they had been waiting for him and were awed by his presence.

Michele sat at his feet, leaning against his knee, quite aware of the elements of composition her pose presented. However, a frown marred her serenity as she glimpsed Jeanne coming from the house bearing a tray of coffee cups and a steaming percolator. Jeanne's brunette beauty was reinforced by the fact that she was a promising artist and was the master's acknowledged protégé.

Paco began to recover his good humor, and forgetting that damned book of Carla's he allowed himself to be drawn into the conversation which seemed to be dealing with the politics of their host country. He took a perverse pleasure in deviating the trend old Henry Parks was taking, and confused the issue for several minutes, taking exactly the reverse side of an argument with which he previously had agreed in principle.

The pleasant French-speaking group on the beautiful lawn seated around the large table under the flowered giant umbrella would have seemed uncomplicated enough to the casual observer, but only the participants knew the inner struggle for their brand of status, a struggle often resembling internecine warfare at its most subtle. The focusing of Paco's attention upon one of them was the goal -- and endless chivvying for position within a group that already had reached high points of achievement.

Oddly enough this international assembly did not include one sycophant. Not one was the least dependent upon Paco for money or hospitality. In fact through either painting or books each had amassed their own admirers. Some had their own villas nearby. It was just that they willingly assumed the role of satellite to Paco's strong sun, bound either to his art or to his political philosophy, which had remained constant throughout the decades. Also with Paco's presence they seemed to strike sparks with the conversation. What Paco lacked in details, he possessed in being the catalyst. He undoubtedly made the electricity.

Paco rose hiking up his blue cotton shorts, and with that gesture called coffee-time to an end. Some would remain on the chance of being invited to dinner -- others would leave and call him back in the evening to see if he wanted a game of chess. In any case they would take a while among themselves, angling to gauge each other's plans prior to making their own.

In the little house by the gate, Pelayo Puig was sorting out the names of visitors whom he deemed worthy of a brief interview with Paco Silva. Pelayo, a dedicated, almost ascetic man was the monk-like secretary who had been with Paco thirty years and still managed to be always in the wrong with his decisions. If he sent an innocuous youth away, clearly wanting an autograph, perhaps to sell, Paco would discover it and complain that he was a "common man" and not everyone he saw needed to be a celebrity. If Pelayo sent in a "common man" he might chide him for wasting his valuable time, of which, he declared, he had little enough time for painting and living his life.

Yet, there was one sure thing Pelayo knew and knew well. Anyone coming in to buy two -- not one, but two -- of the Master's paintings and with American dollars to pay for them was not likely to be turned away. He knew that Paco was always willing to add to his various dollar accounts and here was an excellent opportunity to do that pest of a New York dealer, whom he privately despised, out of a commission. Today, a woman had come calling. Pelayo knew that everything depended upon what attitude the lady took. Any buyer had to strike Paco exactly right.

He examined her closely. Definitely not the Master's type. Good bones, but no soul to the face. More like a mask, than face. The eyes were almost blank -- dead. He imagined that she was some socialite wanting to buy something for the name-dropping value. If Paco were just beginning, he thought, doing the same work as now, he doubted if she would look twice at a Silva. She probably collected only the famous painters and simply lacked a Silva.

"I will have to see if the Master has anything here to sell," he told her guardedly. "He rarely sells from his studio. There is a New York dealer, you know."

"I've seen those," Miss Bennett lied. "In fact, I've been waiting two years for something special. I want two pictures. If possible, related in some way.

"You're not suggesting a pair -- like a pair of lamps, are you?" he bridled.

"Not at the price I'm prepared to pay," she countered. "Naturally, I'll be happy if I can get anything."

Pelayo subsided, mollified by this show of proper humility and placed her name at the top of his list in his precise and deliberate characters. Even though she might not be simpatica to the Master's personality, still it was clear that she knew what she wanted and was prepared not to quibble about it. An ideal buyer. The Master would kill him if he let her go. Besides, she did speak passable Spanish and that was in her favor. Even though he, Pelayo, was a Catalan with his own preferred language, Spanish was quite acceptable to him. He reflected that so few of these socialites spoke more than their own language, and French - - a language he also knew well -- but he appreciated her knowing Spanish, bypassing the so-called chic of the French.

"If you will leave your address and telephone, I can contact you and we will see if something here might please you," he told her loftily.

"That is very kind of you. I'm here for the rest of the winter, quite nearby. Third villa down the road." She gave him a name and added the address and telephone. As she prepared to leave, she asked, "You don't mind or don't think the Master will mind if I pay you in cash? It's a terrible nuisance, but I'm having a little tax trouble at the moment, and there are some dollars I don't want to run through my account."

"Of course," he murmured, "I understand." This was getting better and better. A respectable amount of taxless dollars would be quite welcome to Paco. Art was all well and good, and both he and, of course, Paco, deferred to it, but there was also something to be said for cold cash.

Perhaps she was a little more <u>simpatica</u> than he at first had thought. He deigned to give her a small parting smile, and she left, unaware of the magnitude of this concession.

CHAPTER 3

The thick envelope Maria had placed on her dressing table did not surprise her. Nor did she futilely ask who the messenger was knowing that it could have been delivered to the house by anyone -- boy, man, woman, or mail. Her only concern involved her instructions, which as usual were brief. There was a list of her escape route should that become necessary. A map of the house was included. She was also told that there would be a further message from her contact -- named Tancat. A smaller envelope within contained a million dollars in fresh bills to be used "if necessary" to buy pictures. She was aware of the underlined "if necessary."

The call came a week later. She was to be given what by Pelayo's tone of voice implied was an audience with the living legend, Paco Silva.

"And please be punctual," he had advised. "The Master's time is quite valuable."

"And quite short," she said to herself, but she answered in the expected manner.

"You can imagine my gratitude. If anything, I shall be early."

"Oh, no!" he protested. "That's worse than being late. Do not be early or late. Just be punctual."

Reassurances were given, and now while dressing, she almost smiled, remembering Mr. Gerard, her New York hairdresser, who had often told her that his talent really ran to high fashion in dress design. To prove it, he had, in his meager spare time, run up a gem of a dress of soft Irish linen, sleeveless and simple; it was clear that a master had cut it for it was a small masterpiece of line. Mr. Gerard had insisted that she accept a hand-wrought silver belt decorated with raised gold studs. The matching necklace, also from Mr. Gerard, carried a similar design.

"I couldn't let you wear my dress without the proper accessories," he had confided. "You're a good customer and you do appreciate me. Furthermore, you've got the figure for it -- my creation."

The thin belt and necklace could have been mistaken for costume jewelry; only the initiated would know them as genuine, and that had intrigued her as had the inside finish of the garment. Mr. Gerard had lovingly doubled and pressed every seam within. She thought only she knew the difference of the feel and hang of it.

But the Maestro also knew -- the moment he looked at her. His artist's eye took in her presentation for almost a full moment. She sat across from him in one of the armchairs in his small receiving study, as he had named it. There was only a desk, two armchairs, and a tile floor, but there hung several of his own paintings and two Matisses. He had decided the room needed nothing else -- no gilding of the lily, just the necessary.

Pelayo had retired after his brief introduction. She had run the gamut of hostile eyes as her car entered the gates. The group at the umbrella table had an unspoken nervousness about any new additions to their closed circle. As she walked from the driveway into the house, they paused in their conversation and silently evaluated her. One or two felt a presentiment that the Maestro would in some way become involved. An unspoken antipathy reigned -- in all breasts but one.

Inside, neither Miss Bennett nor Paco Silva rushed into conversation. He narrowed his eyes as though testing perspective then made a frame of his hands.

"Lilac and silver," he finally said in his rather harsh voice, "Good with the shining black hair, gray eyes -- they reflect the silver."

She looked questioningly at him.

"Thin," he continued as though speaking to himself, "and maybe hollow. Do you breathe? Are you alive? Maybe I see a walking mannequin. But it interests me -- there is something else I don't see at this time."

"I -- I'm overwhelmed," she replied at this unforeseen reaction.

"And that's strange," he went on, ignoring her comment, "because you send out nothing of sex appeal as the Americans put it. Absolutely nothing. If I drew you or painted you, it would have to be the way you are. I think you would be angry."

She managed to smile. "I'd be enormously flattered." This interview was taking a strange turn. They had not even mentioned the purchase of pictures.

Paco continued his monologue as he drew a sheet of heaving drawing paper toward him. Selecting a crayon, he made swift controlled strokes as he spoke. "I see this woman," he frowned as he worked, "Ice cold. You must have silver inside too. The face in complete repose. I suppose you have modeled?"

"No," she replied, still surprised, "I was a music teacher."

"Strange," he replied, concentrating on his drawing. "I don't feel those vibrations."

"I don't teach anymore."

They were silent again as he continued drawing. Meanwhile, she tried to take advantage of the time to do some analysis of her own. Strong face, short thick body -- that of a Spanish peasant. Thick vibrant skin, strong muscular shoulders and arms, easy to see since he wore no shirt. His sturdy legs were visible through the opening of his desk. Above all she noted that he filled the room. The personality she felt was almost incandescent and she could begin to understand the impact he made upon the Western world -- a fame which, quite apart from his genius, existed. The press always attended him. His political pronouncements, his new paintings, the enormous sums given for occasional sales of his old paintings, his hobbies, his mistresses, all duly recorded throughout three decades, attention rarely accorded any of his colleagues though also geniuses.

If he would give me another invitation, let me see some of his paintings that could be my first step, she reasoned to herself. Yet it might be too much to hope for. How easy it was for the anonymous them to instruct her to penetrate his circle which she sensed could be as difficult as penetrating a brick wall. And where was Tancat, by the way? What was Tancat doing to help her besides delivering a map and some money -- the million?

She had read the book by his ex-mistress and she felt she knew some of his foibles, but under the circumstances they might have been exaggerated.

"I already have two of your paintings," she ventured.

"Which ones?" he asked, still working at the drawing."

"Your earlier period -- a clown, and the other is the head of a woman."

He thought for a moment. "Did the clown have two eyes in the usual places?"

"Yes, and so did the woman -- a seated woman."

"Ah, I remember. Yes -- my earlier period. The boy was my nephew. I wondered who had that one. The woman seated could have been one of a dozen I worked on during that time."

"And I was hoping to buy two more if you would permit," she continued. "One in your present style, of course."

"Hmmm," he grunted, holding the drawing a little away from him. "This might be good in oils -- but I'm working on something else at the moment." He still seemed to be talking to himself. Suddenly he pushed it towards her over the desk. As he had warned, she did not recognize herself nor at first did she see anything of a woman's head. Only after longer study did the picture evolve. And then she realized it was two drawings in one. First was the outer structure of the face then came almost the optical illusion of the skull beneath. She was impressed and still uncomfortable. This sensitive artist had apparently seen her as an angel of death. And what more could he presage?

"You're not only a genius," she said quietly, "Of course, all the world knows that. But you have the insight of the Gods!" She meant every word.

As this was an accolade never before given him among the many he had harvested, he basked visibly in the warm glow of a new sense of well-being. He knew sincerity when he heard it. His ego was fed. The day had been especially trying. One of his pet theories had been toppled by one of his friends during coffee time. It had been toppled by sheer logic, which he had always hated. Logic in any form always antagonized him. His theories of government were usually emotionally inspired, and as such should be respected; he should have been recognized, he felt, as an authority on all aspects of Communism. Furthermore his work had not gone well that day, fate having added insult to injury.

And now, as in an old silent movie, out of a purple sunset against the background of the purple mountains in the far landscape, had come this strange being wearing lilac and silver. He had almost forgotten that she wanted to buy pictures; at the moment it was more stimulating to draw this face and figure. The crayons he was using so rapidly were almost speaking to him. They were developing his theme so readily that it seemed almost a mistake not to do her in oils. Definitely in oils. Something strange crossed his mind. It would be the first time he had been this interested in painting a woman who by no means attracted him physically.

"I'll see what I have on hand that might do," he told her, rising. "Maybe you can return tomorrow, and I will get Pelayo to show you around the studio."

"Of course I'll come back," she replied, also rising. "I can speak to him on my way out."

"I'm inviting you to supper," he said, leading the way to the door. "If I am going to paint you in oils, I shall need more time with you. This drawing is just an impression. I shall have to make others to decide just what I am going to do."

Only long experience helped her to maintain her poise. Luck was falling into her lap. To be painted by Paco Silva. What a coup! And what an opportunity.

"I am truly flattered, Maestro," she said, following him from the room. "What can I say? Words are not adequate..." she trailed off into platitudes as they left.

CHAPTER 4

The supper of which Silva had spoken corresponded to the important continental diner or American dinner. He conformed to European customs as a rule, ignoring the Mexican heavier meal earlier and light supper later. Keeping Spanish hours, his household ate the important meal at ten in the evening. Tonight, it seemed as though his entire group was to be present -- an event happening once a month.

On being told this, Miss Bennett again blessed her luck for she realized she could sum up the entire coterie individually at practically one sitting.

She was left in the charge of an employee and was ushered into a long low-ceilinged beamed room beautifully lit with colonial candlesticks. Silver gleamed on the long lace-covered table. The carved high-backed chairs spoke of long departed viceroys. Somewhere in another room, someone was playing the piano, and to her practiced hear, it sounded professional.

"There is not much formality here," the lady was saying. "Just a little but the Maestro always insists on everything being beautiful -- that's of most importance to him. That's his rule."

Miss Bennett looked at her in re-evaluation.

"I am the Mistress of the keys," the woman told her, interpreting her look. "I have been in charge of the villa from the first day they came! Ama de las llaves." Having received the proper reaction to this, she continued, "They will come in a moment or two. If you wish, you can sit on this couch and read some magazines -- we have them all -- French, Spanish -- English..."

At this moment several of the group drifted in, still animatedly in discussion of a point earlier examined at their coffee time. Beyond a perfunctory greeting they paid scant heed to Miss Bennett as she sat on a comfortable couch and selected a magazine from the many on the long table in front. She noticed that the women were beautifully gowned and that the men wore white dinner jackets.

Everything changed as Paco, now fully clothed and also in the white jacket though with open shirt, bustled in, accompanied by Michele on one arm and Jeanne on the other. It was a stunning picture, no one could fail to note. The two girls, astonishingly pretty with their light makeup, one very blonde, the other dark, could easily have been models. They set off the imposing presence of Paco who casually greeted everyone, sent the girls to their places, nodded to the others and turned to Miss Bennett to seat her at his right.

She obeyed, and was conscious that the invisible music had grown softer, but continued in a semi-classical vein. Only on the entrance of Pelayo was she presented to everyone. Paco was busy rearranging the seating of some of the others and changing the position of a small flower arrangement on the table. Finally, with

Pelayo at the foot of the table, Paco took his place at the head, and eight sat down for dinner.

Ignoring the rather cold stares of Jeanne and Michele, Miss Bennett kept a low profile, answering only when spoken to. She methodically began to sum up the members of what she privately had designated as the Distinguished Order of Paco Silva's Garter-Group.

There was Henry Parks, on sabbatical from a prestigious Northeastern university where he was Professor of Political Science. His large rather clumsy body bespoke of little exercise with its flabby skin, pot stomach and hunched shoulders. Without the double chin, he could have been thought handsome of face which was set off by short, thick graying hair, almost balancing his physical defects. Next to him was Pierre Duval, a well-known French artist who had, with his lesser-known artist wife, Cecile, pulled up roots from the Riviera to rent a place near Paco. The couple invariably addressed the group in French, as did the others, but all occasionally dropped into Spanish, mainly, she suspected, to show off to Paco that they knew something of what he too told them was "God's Language."

Miss Bennett reflected that Duval was what could be cast in the cinema as the typical French artist. About forty, handsome, still-black hair a little long, falling occasionally over his eyes to be impatiently brushed away. She remembered having seen some of his work in the New York galleries. Cecile, his wife, was obviously in the process of a writing project as she had markedly placed a small notebook beside her plate, then drawn out a small gold pencil from her beaded evening bag, and began peering at Paco. She was an intense woman of around thirty-five, Miss Bennett judged, regular features supported by good bones; her hair, very black with a white feather in front, was severely drawn back in a large bun. The harlequin glasses she wore were held by a guard chain. Miss Bennett was reminded of the classic French woman -- well dressed, talented and soignée.

Her gaze turned to Pelayo, whom she felt she almost knew. There he sat, his pince-nez gleaming efficiently at all and sundry but his air of anticipation proclaimed him ready to devote himself to a good dinner.

The last guest she was able to evaluate was Antonio Murillo, a Spanish matador, famous for his artistic and daring work both in Spain and in Mexico. He was undoubtedly handsome in a rugged manner -- blond with blue eyes -- having been born in San Sebastian in the north of Spain. Contrary to the stereotype of the movie matador, Miss Bennett noted that he joined in the conversation and commented intelligently on a variety of subjects. She had witnessed his arrogant demeanor with the bulls in the rings of Spain, how he had dared death aesthetically. Now all that was missing. Murillo was casual and it was Paco who often addressed him with some point concerning the Fiesta Brave -- the bullfight. Paco's <u>aficion</u> was famous. He had done many stylized pictures of bulls and their matadors.

"Antonio," Paco was now saying, "When I paint you, I will have to paint your hair in black. Who can accept a blond matador?"

"There are enough of us," Antonio laughed, "And two or three right here in Mexico. The Moros for instance, father and son. As a matter of fact, the son is a platinum blond."

Only Paco was interested in the bulls and the conversation usually returned to politics. Talk about painting was deliberately avoided, as it seemed that the artists present prided themselves on not talking shop at dinner.

Paco spoke to Miss Bennett only twice, but she caught his silent regard several times. Even while eating and speaking to others, she felt he was aware of her and thinking of his future painting. Though neither Michele nor Jeanne addressed a word to her she was aware also of their covert attention.

The dinner, combining continental and Mexican cuisine, was not elaborate, but well cooked and seasoned. After the dessert, fruit and coffee, Paco led them into the large adjoining living room where he headed for the onyx chess table. Both Henry Parks and Pierre Duval politely finessed the chair opposite. Paco sat before the set and accepted a liqueur from Jeanne and a strong Mexican cigarette from Michele, which she lighted for him.

Miss Bennett also accepted a liqueur and noted that Henry Parks had out-maneuvered Pierre Duval for a game with Paco. Pierre, drawing up a chair beside the Maestro, kept face by lighting a cigar and declaring he would lead the Maestro to a decisive victory over Henry.

Almost ignored by the others, Miss Bennett sipped the liqueur and mentally added her findings. The girls amused her -- their pique was so obvious; Paco and his kingly, less than benevolent reign interested her. The almost reverent attention paid by all surprised her. How could they maintain their adulation when each was or could be a leader in his field of choice? Even the two girls must have had other opportunities. They were beautiful, also intelligent.

Her thoughts were interrupted when Antonio Murillo sat beside her and offered a cigarette. She accepted and used the opportunity to tell him she had seen him fight the previous season in Madrid. He immediately warmed to her, telling her how he had recently left the infirmary after a goring and had lost three engagements because of it.

"I'm appearing in Plaza Mexico in two weeks," he added. "I hope you will come to see me. Paco will come. They'll all come if he does, but I see you know more about the bullfight -- the Fiesta Brava -- than any of the others -- except Paco, of course. He's a Spaniard -- and an Andalucian besides! But the rest..." he dismissed them with a shrug.

Cecile Duval came to share the sofa, with only a nod to them, she drew out her little book and began scribbling. "So many facets to the Maestro," she murmured, "it's so challenging!"

"I don't understand," Antonio glanced at her notebook, "You seem to be writing all the time."

Cecile's eyes flashed. "Do you realize the importance of this book?" she demanded. "This is going to be the <u>definitive</u> biography."

"But what about your own painting?" he asked. "Doesn't it interfere?"

"You don't understand," she replied, rising abruptly. "Nobody understands except Pierre. My own work can wait, of course." She marched away to take photographs of the chess players with a small camera drawn from her bag.

"I admire and esteem the Maestro," Antonio said turning to Miss Bennett, "but they worship him."

"I have noticed," she replied. "And now when I finish this welcome Spanish cigarette you were so kind to offer me, I must take my leave. I've kept my chauffeur waiting long enough."

As unobtrusively as possible, she said her goodbyes but did not dare interrupt the chess players. Pelayo escorted her to the car and instructed her to report to the Maestro on the following Friday.

"That will give him time to select and prepare a canvas, and to establish the concept. You realize that he has been mulling it over all evening. I can tell -- but to the others he's playing the part of the good host."

She nodded and as he seemed to expect more appreciation, she added, "I will be here Friday -- and on time. Thank you for arranging it."

He handed her into the car with his small smile, and politely watched as it drove off.

As she settled back and took a last look at the villa and grounds, she thought about her unusual evening and was aware that somewhere in there at that very moment sat Tancat.

"One of the servants gave me this envelope for you, Señora," Pepe said passing it over his shoulder- "I told him you were in the villa, but he seemed to want me to give it to you."

She took the envelope and slipped it in her bag. On arriving, she waited until she was alone in her bedroom before opening and reading the contents. On a small slip of paper was written, "Good work." It was signed, "Tancat."

Her instinct had been right. Somewhere in Paco's own home Tancat lurked. But why the anonymity? Her understanding was that he was her aid. She did not at all like the unnecessary mystery he or she seemed to enjoy. There was no need for it at all. Tancat was supposed to ease her path in any way possible, to be the local key -- the indicator.

Yet she did not worry too much, for her luck had been phenomenal. To be painted by Paco Silva gave her every opportunity. It was possible she did not need Tancat at all.

The following day she lounged by the pool with Emily, who, as usual, was chasing low-flying insects, giving special attention to the butterflies. The sun glinted on the water, which constantly changed patterns in the soft breeze. In her swimsuit, a wide-brimmed straw hat tilted over the eyes, a daiquiri at her side, she drifted between sleeping and waking. Somewhere beyond the high walls of the villa came the muted snatches of laughter and occasional singing from the casual passers-by. She surrendered herself to sleep, as time seemed to stand still. Emily, too, stretched out on the warm tiles pleasantly fatigued and promptly drowsed.

A shadow intruded as Yolanda, barefoot, had silently approached. "Señora, inside there is a visitor for you -- a man -- but he is a <u>gentleman</u>," she assured her, implying that she knew the difference between a man and a gentleman -- just a man, of course, would never have been admitted. "Maria gave him a lemonade in the entrance until I could see if you wanted to receive him or not."

Slowly she gathered her thoughts from never-never land, reached for her short beach robe and with an effort rose and stretched. This just might be Tancat, she thought. Perhaps he was from Paco's enclave. Perhaps her contact.

"I'll dress," she finally replied. "Show him into the living room and I'll come down shortly."

She changed quickly and in minutes descended to confront a stranger who rose to greet her. Tall, broad-shouldered with what to others would have been an infectious smile, he approached her, hand outstretched.

"Mrs. Duran?" he inquired and affirmed at the same time, "Yes, it's Mrs. Duran, I think."

"I am," she replied, appreciating his good Eastern accent in English.

"I'm really repentant to horn in on you like this," he said easily -- too easily for real repentance. "Please don't think I'm collecting for charity or anything like that -- it's just that -- may I sit a moment?" he waved her to a chair before taking one himself.

"I'm Greg Benton, a neighbor. It's just that we, in the American colony her, are organizing a Little Theatre Group, and when word got around of a newcomer, and a grand possibility of an addition to our project, I was delegated to contact you."

There was a pause as she deliberately waited to respond. About the last thing she wanted on this or any assignment was matriculation in any such organization. Anonymity or as much of it as she could arrange was her primary necessity. Quite aside from this was her habitual withdrawal from unnecessary contact with anyone, and even if she did have a "social" assignment, she not then nor ever wished to be a part of what she thought was a frivolous, hard-drinking, hell-bent-for-happiness search group in the area. She preferred to be left alone in absolute luxury with her cat.

As she studied him she found it easy to imagine his theatrical participation as a leading man -- about thirty-six, rather good looking, heavy chestnut hair, a smile calculated to charm- He was dressed in tailored buff-colored cotton trousers and an open neck shirt; his physique spoke of the athlete -- of daily workouts.

"I know this is rather sudden," he added, aware of her hesitation, "but here is a summary of our past and future goals." He handed her a printed folder which she started reading.

"I'm not too sure..." she began, knowing full well she had not the remotest idea of participating in his group.

"But we don't do anything like Ibsen or Shakespeare," he hastened to assure her, "just light stuff -- fun things -- musicals, and the most serious thing we ever tried was Pinero and some Oscar Wilde. You'd fit in so well. We need your type."

"My type?"

"Well, yes," he rejoined immediately. "Sophistication -- high style -- high adventure spies -- all that sort of thing..." he trailed off still smiling. "I certainly hope you'll think it over." he ended.

She pretended to read the folder, preparing, meanwhile, the reply designed to rid herself of him as quickly and definitely as possible.

Permitting her time for scanning the material, he took a casual look around. "What a great house," he commented as she finished reading. "I have a nearby house too, but it's one of those modern affairs -- and just big enough for one. Good patio, though. That's where I work. I'm a magazine writer, doing a series on Mexican cities."

"Oh, a writer? How interesting." she said placing the folder on a nearby table. "Mr. Benton, was it?"

"Yes, Benton," he replied, "but please call me Greg -- and don't turn me down."

She smiled slightly and began anew. "Well, Greg, it's just that I've recently lost my husband, and I don't feel I'm quite ready for this sort of thing at the moment."

"Oh, I'm sorry, please forgive me." This time he did sound repentant.

"But I want to subscribe," she continued. "I see that you could use more patrons. Count me in for my share."

"You're a love," his face lighted up. "And if you can just come out to the meetings, we'll be happy -- and maybe to the rehearsals."

"I don't have my checkbook handy at the moment, but I'll send my contribution to the address on the folder," she said rising in dismissal.

He was forced to rise also but lingered a moment. "We really appreciate this. Your name will go on all programs as a sponsor."

"Don't bother -- I'm not important."

"No way," he replied, "no way. Could you give me your full name, please? I'll jot it down."

"Mrs. Frederick J. Duran," she replied. "If you insist."

She followed him from the house to the large garden doors noting that his manner seemed more subdued, as if in respect for her recent widowhood.

"And I hope you'll let me invite you over one afternoon to my place," he add pausing at the gates. "No fuss -- what I mean is just a small sort of afternoon -- small drinks, small dinner later, and home all safe and sound before midnight." Not waiting for a reply, he shook her hand and got into his Corvette parked in front and sped off down the narrow cobblestone road in a flurry of dust.

She was grateful he had not asked for her telephone number and planned to warn Pepe and Maria not to admit him again. She went in to lunch and as she sat at the long table, a half-awakened memory surfaced. Deep down in thoughts she usually successfully suppressed stirred the memory of her dead husband -- the real one. And this, she thought, was very strange because the man so recently departed was nothing like him at all.

CHAPTER 5

Friday arrived. Pelayo with many instructions met her at the gate. She had earlier been told to wear the same dress and accessories. She must not engage the maestro in conversation, but was to respond briefly to any comment of his. She was to keep absolutely still during the painting intervals which might be short or long, depending on how the work was going. During her rest periods she must not look at the work in progress, nor mix with any of the other guests because this might change her entire aura. She would not be paid, of course, but the maestro would present her with one of the drawings as a gift of appreciation.

She nodded agreement as they entered. As it was early, there was no group to pass at any of the lawn tables. Neither Jeanne nor Michelle was in sight.

The studio was awe-inspiring. Though three stories in height, it still created an air of intimacy, which was surprising. The slanted skylight, the various pieces of sculpture, two easels with unfinished works, several rough sketches pinned on cork walls, vases, some with fresh flowers, others with faded ones. She also noticed several mugs of cold, unfinished coffee on some of the large carved tables.

"The maestro doesn't let anyone touch anything." Pelayo spoke sotto-voce as though in church. "He doesn't even let the cleaning woman in -- oh maybe once a month."

"The tiled floors are beautiful," she commented.

"The tiles are straight from Spain," he proudly answered. "Especially designed by the maestro!"

"Where is he, by the way?" she asked still examining the studio.

"He will be here in good time. Just sit here a moment -- facing the light so he can decide. Yes, that's about right." He adjusted her position as though he himself were the prospective artist.

The door to the garden opened and Paco stood for a moment in the entrance. He wore the same faded blue shorts as before, was barefoot and shirtless which seemed his daytime custom. He ignored Pelayo and gave her only brief acknowledgement, staring into her face, then backing away still gazing. He finally approached her elevated chair to turn her head at several angles, as though she were an inanimate doll. Pelayo left the room and Paco, apparently having decided upon the pose, began work on the large prepared canvas, stopping only once to raise her chair about two inches. He then touched a button on the wall and to her surprise a Beatles record played softly and he began to hum along as he worked, apparently familiar with the music and words.

Time passed and with it she began to feel an overpowering boredom accompanied by strained and tiring muscles. Fully aware of the many who would have given their all to be in her place, she nevertheless longed for the promised rest period. After what seemed to her an hour, but in reality was only half, Paco threw down his brushes and with a grunt padded off through the garden door for coffee with his waiting group. Very shortly Jeanne entered the studio with a tray containing sandwiches and cafe filtre, which was gratefully accepted. She ate while pacing the floor to rest cramped muscles. Jeanne lingered, glancing from her to the maestro's work. Finally she broke the silence.

"You should be extremely happy," she spoke in French, smiling a little condescendingly. "The Maestro hasn't done women for several years." The derogatory tone she placed on "women" was marked.

"I am," she replied in English in an effort to end the conversation, almost sure she would not be understood. She also well knew that a servant could have brought the refreshment tray.

Jeanne hesitated, took another look at the canvas and left the room with a toss of her dark, shoulder-length hair.

Miss Bennett, gratefully alone, examined more closely the sacred precincts. The painting did not in the least interest her. She wanted to think of the elements of her work -- at the moment, and of escape possibilities. There were three doors strategically placed, four large curtain-less windows giving on to various parts of the garden.

The locked garden gate, usual in the area, was always a factor, she knew. Now this is where her invisible contact could be useful. And what was the full inside layout of the house? The short time she had spent in the dining room had told her very little. Like many of the old houses in the city the design would be of a rambling, unpredictable structure. The earlier map had proved quite sketchy.

These thoughts were interrupted by Paco who again padded in and without a word, readjusted her pose, stared at her for a full two minutes, and began his work. To her surprise, the tape now changed into a Bach fugue which he also hummed.

At last after two more rest periods, similar to her first one, Paco again threw his brushes down, carefully lowered his palette and sighing noisily, called an end to the session.

"I never knew that just sitting still could be so tiring," she ventured as she stretched and got to her feet.

"Yes, some say it can be a chore," he replied flopping into a director's chair in front of the painting. He peered critically at it.

"I remember you wanted something of mine that's finished," he spoke still looking at the canvas. "Nothing in here, of course, is for sale. I am really working on everything you see here. Maybe they look finished, but they're not. In one of my other studios -- the one Michele works in, Pelayo can take you there to see if you like something." He paused and looked at her. "You will be here at the same time tomorrow, of course."

She inwardly smiled at his confidence. "Of course, Maestro," she replied.

That night, she was satisfied to find a complete plan of Paco's villa in a sealed envelope on her dressing table. Upon questioning, Maria told her that a young man whom she, Maria, did not know, had delivered it after dinner while the Señora had been taking her evening swim.

The plan showed a crude penciled outline of the rooms and garden. The first page showed a map of the rambling first floor and the second page included the second floor and grounds. The symbols were written in English, rather brief and very neat. Idle curiosity prompted her to speculate on her contact who still so coyly insisted on remaining anonymous.

It could be either of the girls, perhaps driven by a secret jealousy against the man who could so openly maintain relationships with both. Could one or both of them have rebelled? Together with their undeniable beauty -- the classic blonde and the classic brunette, they were both above average in intelligence, she had noticed, as they held their own with the others in the dinner conversation. She could not underestimate them by any means.

And wasn't there something rather overdone about Cecile Duval's dedication to Paco? Something rather dramatic as though she was trying to lay the groundwork, to establish her loyalty in front of a judge and jury. There would be many witnesses in her favor -- how she had suspended her own work -- how she went around with her little book and gold pencil always scribbling or snapping photos of her subject almost every half hour. What motive would she have?

And what about her husband, Pierre, who had moved from the Riviera to be near his friend. Was that quite usual? Was there some hidden resentment in the worldwide fame of a colleague which overshadowed his own work?

Then there was Henry Parks, the typical absent-minded professor on sabbatical leave, immersed in his theories of ideal government, spouting them incessantly, arguing about Communism -- he against, Paco emotionally for, maintaining his original stand and expecting to be invited by the Kremlin's die-hards to lend strength and status to their views. She had garnered this by the dinner conversation. It was impossible not to listen to the animated and sometimes explosive exchanges of viewpoints, relieved only by Paco's occasional attention to Antonio Murillo.

And what about Murillo? She knew that a matador in the top category rarely dipped into politics of any country, but could there be a personal hidden vendetta? It would be wise not to discount Antonio Murillo -- until more could be known. After all, they were the only two Spaniards in the group. Except for American Henry Parks, the rest were French.

At last she considered Pelayo -- a most likely candidate -- the least suspected, but with ample opportunity. So dry, so precise, so didactic but who knew what years of frustration the secretary had endured? It could be pent up. He was probably underpaid if

Carla's book could be believed as it touched upon Paco's parsimony. But it was clear that Pelayo was talented. How efficiently had he arranged the pose in that chair this morning. How meticulous he had been.

Later, preparing for bed, she cleared her mind with a practiced discipline. What did it really matter who had planned the hit? She had usually avoided all interest in the motives of her previous assignments. She had one objective and must not forget it. Hers was not to reason why, she told herself as she turned to the Nineteenth Century anthology of poetry which she had packed for moments like these. Only a few more details to be sealed and she could act. Then back to New York with Emily to her very own island on the highest floor of the building -- her own island with its solitude -- until her next assignment, of course.

That night was perfect for slumber. The usual soft breeze gently moved the diaphanous curtains. Emily was curled snugly in her corner of her own bed and the radio was carrying the broadcast of the Huapango played by the Symphony Orchestra of Mexico City. Miss Bennett's spirits rose as she remembered the new nightgown she had brought -- the rose chiffon with the criss-cross narrow satin ribbons -- a morale builder, the final touch. The four silken floating layers enveloped her as she adjusted herself between the sheets against her four down pillows stacked behind her back and shoulders. This established, she read the poetry far into the night.

In the week that followed she received two telephone calls, that true to the law of coincidences came within ten minutes of each other.

"Hi there, remember me?" came the first voice. "I'm Greg Benton."

She suppressed her exasperation. "Yes, Mr. Benton, of course I remember."

"Just a reminder. We're having a dress rehearsal tonight. Thought I'd let you know. I can come by and pick you up. I thought if you..."

"But I don't think..."

"Oh nothing really big. It's just our own little group. And I want you to see your name on the program -- it's with the sponsors."

"I specifically asked that it not be," she replied stiffly.

"No big deal," he laughed. "Don't be modest. Anyway I'm picking you up at eight- thirty. Thanks for the hundred you sent us." He rang off abruptly to her dismay. How could she swat an annoying gnat who labored under the illusion he was some TV sitcom protagonist with a way with women. And how did he acquire her telephone number, and what would be the best way to snub him definitively?

A loud ring of the phone still in her hand interrupted these questions. It was the call she had expected for some time. The familiar voice, one of two she could recognize, never, however, having seen the owner of either, spoke to her with a marked economy of words. A safe house, passports, and a "soft kill" were mentioned. "In case of necessity," she was told. She did not speak of her good luck in posing for her target, but she mentioned the fact that her presumed contact had not surfaced except for written communication. There was no comment on this, which did not surprise her, as she knew the information would be transferred to higher echelons. The conversation ended after she received an emergency number and the time that number would be covered. She was glad to see this did not conflict with her sittings.

She was careful to be punctual for these with her makeup and coiffure exactly the same, and of course, the dress. A call to Mr. Gerard and Federal Express had successfully yielded a duplicate together with a glowing letter from him congratulating them both on the impact of the dress, and underlining the fact that this encouraged him greatly in going over to haute couture.

During her sittings she felt a new respect for artists' models. Only they could know the boredom, the vacant space in one's life, the tiring muscles, sometimes cramping. As for her, what really was the use? The need for this constant sitting when the man's style was plainly and starkly impressionistic -- he had, in fact, embraced it right up there in the vanguard, turning from his representational style as soon as possible. She weighed the advantage of access to the house -- the convenience -- the possibilities -- as not always was it necessary to use her twenty-two.

Cutting short these reflections she hurried to her room to prepare for her ten o'clock sitting, yielding to a strange sort of discipline which she herself failed to understand.

As she entered the walk up to the studio, she nodded briefly to the group assembled under their usual umbrella at their usual table awaiting Paco's morning break. Antonio Murillo was absent because of his daily training schedule, but present were the Duvals, Henry Parks, Michele and Jeanne. Pelayo was in his office, dealing with the correspondence and the various facets of running the villa.

After Miss Bennett's passing, Michele turned to the group to express her mounting resentment. "I fail to see the attraction of that lady, Mrs. Duran," she doused her cigarette firmly for emphasis. You two are artists; do her features have something out of the common mold? Where is her attraction?"

The Duvals, so addressed, hesitated as they exchanged knowing glances. Finally Pierre answered. "There are things the Maestro sees beyond the surface. That's why he is world famous."

"The woman does have some kind of mystique," Cecile declared. "She isn't beautiful like you, but I can easily understand her attraction -- as an artist, of course."

Jeanne, annoyed at not having been thus categorized and included in the in-group of the two artists present, considered her position. Her problem was that inwardly she agreed with Michele, but as a matter of policy she elected to take the opposing side.

"As an artist myself," Jeanne began, pausing for effect.

"Ha!" scoffed Michele, casually gazing into the distance.

"As I was saying," Jeanne continued, ignoring her, "as an artist and protégé of the Maestro, I think I know more about his taste than most."

Cecile, who was scribbling in her ever-present notebook, paused, as did Pierre who drew on his cigar and leaned back, enjoying the exchange.

Jeanne continued, having just thought of an idea to augment her stand. "It could be the planes of her face that intrigue the Maestro, because they coincide with the manner in which he draws faces in any case. She personifies his style of painting. He has encountered his technique in a living person."

"Not a bad summary, Jeanne," Pierre nodded, surprised. "You just might have hit it."

"Of course one couldn't expect a non-artist to understand -- it's rather a subtle point - - would be to them," Jeanne basked under Pierre's support.

"Are you working on something at the moment?" Cecile asked, at last putting away her pen and booklet.

"Paco doesn't like me to work without his supervision, and he's too involved now to give me the time."

"Ha!" repeated Michele still gazing into the middle distance as she selected another cigarette. She ignored Jeanne's quick glare.

"Well, Cecile and I have painted for three hours already this morning and there's always plenty of light in the afternoons in this country," Pierre commented hoping to change the subject.

"But back to this woman," Jeanne continued warming to her newly adopted viewpoint, "There's more to her face than is at first visible. And I have seen the work Paco has started. He's painting the outer and inner face at the same time."

"But he has always done that," Cecile replied sharply. "Don't you think so, Henry?" She turned to Henry Parks who had been regarding them indulgently from his academic heights. "You're pretty quiet this morning. What's the matter today?"

"Just listening to you people going around in circles," he smiled. "Why don't you get into the real world?"

"We're already in the real world," all but Michele responded raggedly. They had anticipated a snub from him and were more or less prepared.

"You're taking a busman's holiday on your sabbatical," Pierre said earnestly. "I know you're working on that new book. Political. But all work and no play -- get with it, Henry; try to get some other interests. All you can talk is political science. And frankly, this new thing with Russia has made you even worse!"

Parks demurred, having heard this advice all too frequently. He shrugged it off as usual and poured himself more coffee.

Meanwhile inside, Paco had started work in good spirits surprising himself upon how well this project had gone. He fully realized that some of his enemies had said that he would create a series of linear representations from memory and sell the result for a fortune. But he well knew it was not that simple. His best work was always done from life -- as he saw it. No smears, splashes nor splattering or smudging. No matter what was said behind his back by envious colleagues, he was truth itself as his fame had proven.

Miss Bennett moved her eyes a fraction from the set pose. She looked at the old crusted coffee cups trying to remember when he had last sipped from the cold remains. He seemed to need the caffeine and strong French and Mexican cigarettes. She had, from the beginning, been treated as any paid professional model, left alone in the studio during rest periods, not invited to have coffee with the others, and prohibited from looking at the work in progress. She did not resent all this, but she noticed it. Now at this point, two weeks after her first sitting, she wondered how long the completion of the picture would take, for she had no illusions that there would be more invitations to Casa Silva when it was completed. She sensed that she would shortly be <u>de</u> <u>trop</u>.

CHAPTER 6

She had forgotten about Greg Benton because of the important second call that morning and the exigencies of sitting for Silva. It was a surprise, and not a particularly pleasant one when he appeared at her side in the garden during her evening walk. He was smiling broadly with remarkable assurance considering their short acquaintance.

"Just can't take 'no' for an answer," he joked genially. "I will not let you burrow down in this place alone -- attractive though it may be. Come on -- just as you are now -- just come along to the rehearsal."

Above her protests he gently but firmly urged her along to the gate, which was opened by a smiling Pepe. In a short time she was whisked around the narrow streets, some unpaved, some hilly, some turning almost at right angles, until he drew up in front of a small stone building from which sounds of a musical tuning-up emerged.

"Don't expect too much," he kept repeating, "but I think it might be a passable effort on our group's part."

Feeling completely outdone, she blamed herself for having forgotten to tell Pepe and Maria not to admit him, and decided to make the best of it.

"I'm sure it'll come out just fine," she answered. "But I'm not such good company now. Could I just sit in a corner and watch? I'm not too good with people right through here."

"Now don't you worry. Little by little. You might not believe it, but I know the situation. Trust me!" True to his word he guided her to a side seat near the back and did not introduce her to the rest of the cast. Feeling less pressure because of it, she settled back to watch a reasonable facsimile of "Guys and Dolls."

She saw that Greg was not a bad Sky Masterson. His voice was good and she suspected he had participated in other amateur productions. After a long hectic session marked by several flare-ups of temperament by members of the cast impressed by their sudden importance in the limelight, the rehearsal ended with a sarcastic resume by the director, another professional amateur.

Greg picked her up and on the way to the car asked for her "candid opinion."

"It's really a good production," she responded sincerely, "you're very good indeed. Have you had experience?"

"Only at Princeton, years ago," he laughed. "Triangle production of course."

"It shows," she answered.

He took the complement gracefully and they drove off. Rounding an acute scary turn with ease, he turned to her confidently. "I've prepared a simple little spread for you," he announced.

"I must get home, really," she protested resolving never to be caught in such a web again.

"I know. You're sitting for the great Paco Silva," he said good-humouredly. "Your houseman boasted of it to me. He's proud of you. I guess you don't want to stay up too late -- to be jaded for tomorrow."

She was vaguely annoyed to feel her privacy gradually being chipped away. She must speak to Pepe who obviously liked and approved of this man. She was silent until they reached his house.

He had underestimated it to her. She walked through a garden expertly lit for night guests, and which included an attractive pool. They walked up the path lined by carefully trimmed shrubbery and passing through a large terrace, entered a wide low-ceilinged living room. It seemed especially designed for the utmost in masculine taste and comfort, with large cushioned suede chairs, leather tables, long low bookcases, leather-shaded lamps, and animal-skin rugs thrown over onyx floors.

"I like your decoration," she said looking around. "Quite a place you've got."

"It's home -- a no-frills home," he said going to the bar. "It's comfortable. I'm almost finished paying for it," he laughed.

"Good for you," she smiled, accepting what proved to be a well-made daiquiri noting that he seemed to know her taste in cocktails.

He then clicked a button which activated a lively piece which she immediately recognized as one of her favorite Chopin scherzos.

"Classical music seems to go in cycles too," he commented settling with his drink in a chair opposite hers. He seemed to be careful in keeping his distance as if to prove his good intentions. "Remember the Tchaikovsky ear? Then Chopin -- or was it the reverse?

What next?"

"It's a good trend when it happens in any case," she commented. "Helps the man on the street to know good music." As she spoke she noticed a small grand piano beyond the stereo, and some impulse made her approach it. She checked the brand name -- a French import. Fearing it was out of tune, she softly ran her fingers over the keys to find it perfectly tuned. Benton switched off the tape and waited. Her back was not to him and she sat down slowly at the piano surprised at her own impulse. Then her fingers seemed to take on a life of their own. She began the same scherzo which had been one of her favorites. Something made her look up to a mirror beyond the piano on a far wall. Still playing she caught a quick glimpse of the face of the man standing behind her. The change was startling. Gone was the pleasant expression, the amiable playboy smile. In place was an intensity so surprising that she was almost thrown off the remembered and demanding notes of the music. However, she continued the short difficult piece until its sudden end.

He caught her eye in the mirror afterward and smiled, but she felt she had seen another man in that revealing moment. She rose and picked up her waiting cocktail.

"I'm a little out of practice."

"But that's wonderful!" he explained. "I had no idea -- why you're a pro!"

"Just a lowly music teacher," she shrugged, noticing that he seemed rather disoriented, as though re-evaluating her.

A door opened and a white-coated houseman entered with a tray of hors d'oeuvres. Supper would shortly be served, he told them in Spanish.

"But where did you study?" he insisted after the man left. "You're undoubtedly professional," he repeated.

"Julliard," she said, "but I never played at 'concert pitch'," she smiled hoping to terminate the subject.

"Did you teach in New York?"

"New Jersey," she replied before thinking, and immediately felt a mental warning, having never mentioned that state to anyone. For the rest of the evening she felt the shadow of her involuntary slip.

The next afternoon found Greg Benton sitting on the terrace, drink forgotten beside him, staring unseeingly at the distant volcano now wrapped at the top with a transparent mist. If the thoughts of Miss Bennett concerning Greg Benton had, in the words of the poet, been long long thoughts, his thoughts concerning Mrs. Duran, as he knew her were even longer. At first he was sure he had penetrated her cover. Of all the surveillance he had recently done, her house had been the last he had successfully bugged. The conversation recorded there had been pay dirt, crowning his search of a month, ever since in contact from the Embassy had alerted him to the contract put out for Silva. He had to admire the subtlety of the whole scheme. The influential Silva supports Communism, defends the hardliners, but is liquidated before he can get over to give comfort to them in front of international cameras. This act can be directed to the United States since the Western Hemisphere is dominated by them. So therefore the implication could last throughout the years. There would be no necessity for proof -- just a continuing mystery which would endure as did another similar one years ago in Mexico, also a political murder.

He knew Silva's limitations as a polemist, that he had only surface knowledge of his dedicated position, but he also knew as did the hardliners still in Russia, that fed by the experts with the right material, his dramatic television presence, his charisma could gather many converts back to their old beliefs. He was now considered dangerous by some of his erstwhile friends now wanting him silenced and soon, before the expected

Russian visit. He could be too influential -- tip the still-wavering scales.

Benton was aware that the intervention of his branch of the government was necessary. Well he knew Paco's death would be thrown at Washington's doorstep, as it would be also convenient for them, but in this instance the blame would be unfair. This hit must be blocked. Paco must be convinced to retract publicly and to decline the expected invitation.

And now this woman. That expressionless something in her eyes, her preference for solitude, her knowledge of judo, her interest in the Silva group -- and sitting for the portrait! She could act at any moment. He must at all costs remove Silva from daily risk -- try to convince him as he had vainly done before. It was an uphill chore to deal with such an ego. Sure of his adulation from one and all, including the press, his admirers, and most governments, Paco had laughed at him, dismissing any serious danger and reaffirming the fact that Communism was not entirely dead in Russia, and it was up to him to help reinstate it.

Again his thoughts returned to Miss Bennett. He was at first sure he had impressed her, that she believed his cover, for he really was going to open in the musical, and he really had published three articles on aspects of Mexico in a minor travel magazine. He had considered his cover impeccable. But the dazzler had come -- that piano -- that music. She was more than he had originally thought. There was more intelligence and talent inside in spite of the outside mannequin aspect of her wardrobe. Other indications of a solid cultural background were recalled. Had he not heard her voice on that telephone call, he would doubt the facts he now had to face. If only he could get that report from the New York office which he had immediately demanded after he had taken her home.

What was the Jersey town within commuting distance from New York City? Assuming she had lived in New Jersey while studying in New York. It could have been that she had both lived and studied in New York, but something in the manner in which she had said, "New Jersey" gave him the feeling that it had been her home. In any case it was a start. Computers would help at the office and he thanked God he did not have to go through the numbing boredom of doing that part of the work.

He rose and began the familiar process of steeling himself against any personal or subjective attitudes. Meanwhile he must somehow arrange a more comprehensive guard plan for Silva. Then surfaced the thought he had tried to suppress all afternoon, but now he faced it in all its clarity. If they could not locate, penetrate and break not only the various elements of the hit, but also the New York origin of the arrangers, first, then she would have to be neutralized.

CHAPTER 7

"Just a reminder, we're opening tomorrow," he began when she came to the phone.

"Yes, I know. I remembered," she replied with a cordiality that surprised him.

"Can I pick you up at seven? I've got to be there early. And you can get a better seat since there are no reservations."

"I'll be ready," she replied, "and break a leg, as they say on Broadway."

He laughed and after a further brief exchange, they rang off.

She smiled slightly as she left the phone, gratified that she had now identified the baffling element that made him remind her of some aspect of her late husband. This night will tell the story, she thought. I can verify my theory even if I must confront him directly."

She talked to Maria about a late supper. Then she had Pepe drive her to town to select an outstanding vintage wine and to visit the beauty salon.

The amateur presentation the following night was hailed as a triumph by the audience. Curtain calls were numerous and laudatory reviews would be sure to appear in the English language newspaper as the journalist was seen to be clapping enthusiastically as was the elderly lady who supplied the "around town" column for the same paper. Miss Bennett saw what an accomplished singer and actor Benton really could be. He was a natural, falling into the role even better than in the dress rehearsal.

There were several celebration parties planned for the case, and after the show, when he picked her up, he suggested that they attend one.

"Just for a while -- a few moments," he urged realizing her reluctance.

"Just for a while," she repeated, "because tonight you'll be my guest. I've had a supper prepared." She realized that he would want to savor his success with the others and steeled herself to accompany him to one of the reunions. It was the kind of affair she most disliked, but she gracefully endured listening to recapitulations of the piece, enthused snatches of lines almost forgotten at the time, of the trials of making certain high notes due to the nervous-making opening night.

With a set smile and nursing a drink she pretended to sip, she got through what seemed an eon and sighed with relief when at last they turned in at the gates of her house which were opened by Pepe. Maria and Yolanda had followed her instructions about the lighting and the music, and had outdone themselves with the supper reveling in their first chance to show their mettle. From the onion soup made exactly as it was in France, to the <u>rognons Jerez</u> to the tarte a fruit, the meal was authentically French, and was, duly appreciated, she observed, by him as such.

"Didn't know there was such culinary talent in this town," he commented at the end. "My houseman cooks well, but always the Veracruz cuisine pops up. It's delicious, but there's never a variation."

"I'm lucky," she told him. "It seems the owners of this place sent Maria to the

Cordon Bleu here in Mexico. I get the Mexican and French cuisine alternated."

She had several times congratulated him, listened to his disclaimers, seen his actor's satisfaction when she analyzed the performances of the others, but always returned to the fact that his was the most professional performance.

Even with his several preoccupations concerning his hostess and mission, he was still vulnerable to her evaluation of his performance. He put everything else on hold for the moment and urged her on. She knew whereof she spoke as she had seen the Broadway production and also the film. Her analysis, he thought, was apt and to the point. Glowing in her praise, he allowed himself the luxury of enjoying the moment.

After all, he had worked and rehearsed for weeks and he felt he deserved something.

They left the dining room as she led the way into a smaller room where coffee and liqueurs would be forthcoming. He appreciates its intimacy enhanced by the softly glowing fireplace in front of which were two comfortable armchairs.

"Never mind the Colonial period," he laughed as he sat extending his legs in complete relaxation. "Your hospitality is fabulous -- gourmet food, wine, liqueurs, and a real comfortable chair afterward."

"And something else," she added taking the other chair, "It's story time."

"Story time?"

"Yes, story telling time. I have a little story for you."

He settled back gratefully. The excitement of the acting, the experience of the well-planned dinner, the cocktails earlier at the after-theatre party, now the warmth and comfort of the room with something more to come, it seemed. He lowered what remained of his defenses.

She began, "Once there was a young couple who had saved their money to take one of the reasonable package tours to Europe. They offer them occasionally -- you know, two weeks in three or four countries -- everything included -- tips and all."

He nodded, and suddenly for the first time he began to imagine how pleasant it could be if she were nothing more than a sophisticated attractive woman who so well could have qualified as his type. Similar interests, music, herself an accomplished musician, connoisseurs of good food and drink, always exquisitely dressed. For instance, that dress she now wore could have passed as a cotton print to the average person, but his training and residence in Mexico told him the material had been embroidered solidly in raised designs of flowers. Then the thin flat gold chain with its star sapphire pendant, plain gold earrings -- all understated, but what perfect coordination. How was it possible she could be what he suspected? Against all logical factors, he wished for some plausible explanation.

"And while in Paris this couple came upon this little pharmacy near the Opera section," she was saying.

"Remember the name? I used to know one..." he interrupted.

"I'll never forget it. The Verdi -- Pharmacie Verdi."

"Right! The same. I know it. The owner..."

"Was a nice old man of the old school. Made lots of things from his own recipes..." Her eyes lit up with a rare light.

"Yes, his own recipes -- from scratch as you say, and with the best ingredients..."

She nodded and continued. "My husband and I -- of course it was some years ago, you understand, wandered into this place. It didn't take long for him to see our funds were limited, so he gave us a discount. We liked his products so much, and I guess he appreciated it."

"Oh, he was great! His kind is rare enough now."

"How true," she smiled. "Well, my husband bought a bottle of perfume for me, and I bought a cologne aftershave for him. We loved the fragrance -- what a blend."

"I know. I use it all the time. What a coincidence," he laughed. "I send for it.

Hope to God he's still alive. He had a nephew, you know. He might have taken it over."

"Yes?"

"Yes. Nothing can really compare with that stuff -- really dry!"

"Yes, very dry..." she paused and looked at him. "Unique," she waited.

He sensed a new dimension in the exchange. A dawning awareness came to him, intensifying as he listened to her next words.

"And that unique, very dry fragrance used by the very select few was evident on an intruder the night he arrived in this house."

With difficulty he kept an emotionless face, pausing at the full significance of what she was telling him. He knew he had blithely walked into her trap.

"But this is terrible," he finally answered. "An intruder?" He sat up.

"With very good taste," she replied. "Using the same lotion. I know it so well.

Rather like your height and build."

"Good God!" he exclaimed. "That really makes me mad. It could have been dangerous! I'm going to suggest more security here for you. I insist!" He rose and leaned against the mantel, changing into a more confidential tone." In fact, Mrs. Duran, I was going to speak to you about security in any case. I don't want to scare you, but I think you're in danger here from another source."

"You must be joking!"

"This sleepy little town isn't half of what it seems."

"I know."

"You know? What do you know?"

"First tell me why I'm in danger."

Fully aware of the deadly game they were playing, he was tempted to confront her with facts. Yet he held back, realizing how hazardous it might be to the total picture at this point. The search of her background had been instigated. The New York telephone number she had been given was invaluable, but that too took time to probe. He longed to get to that connection as soon as possible. A quick decision took but a second -- an almost routine part of his job -- the plausible lie.

"Look, I'm going to level with you," he gave her his look of sincerity, trying to ignore her amused smile. I am a writer -- that's for sure. But I make my real money as a private detective working for an agency -- headquarters in Mexico City. My present job is to keep vigil on certain politicians' families here -- you know how they've started kidnapping the wealthy -- robbing their houses --

all that. Paco Silva is one of my clients..." he trailed off, waiting to see her reaction.

"I see," she answered after finishing her liqueur, "but I wouldn't have thought..."

"And frankly," he interrupted, "I was the one who was checking out your house, the same way I've checked several located near the Silva ménage. A necessary precaution. Yes, I was the so-called intruder."

"And what was the need for all the secrecy?" she asked.

"Secrecy is a built-in factor of this kind of work. Without it, I could never have discovered the potential danger that surrounds Paco Silva. Such a figure is ripe for kidnapping, and here you are, sitting for you every day. You could easily become involved.

Leave Mexico please before you do!" he began pacing, but quickly stopped to return to his chair.

"I don't understand the reason," she countered. "I'm not particularly wealthy or famous."

"But you're at the villa almost daily. Anything might explode -- any time."

His sincere tone belied the fact that he knew she was to be the prime mover of that potential explosion. If only he could get her out of the way -- get her to contact her employers, get her off the scene so he would not have to kill her.

As if answering his thought, she spoke. "Did it ever occur to you that you, too, are in danger?"

He was completely taken aback, as the words and the tone held the full impact of a threat. Just who was the pursued and who was the pursuer? This woman might be as dangerous as he, and probably a very good shot. Accustomed as he was to danger, he felt a sudden atavistic fear. She was lethal, and he was realizing it more and more. Yet he managed a deprecating gesture.

"Another liqueur?" she asked indicating the flacon on the side table.

"You seem startled -- are you all right? Maybe I shouldn't have spoken."

He hated himself for the involuntary giveaway. "Perfectly O.K." he smiled. "It's just that you surprised me for a moment. No, nothing more. I have to drive, but please think over what I said, and thanks for coming to the play, and for the great supper."

They rose and said their goodbyes with the customary handshake, and she gave no indication that she had decided to kill him now that she realized he was the prime obstacle in preventing her from doing her job.

She went up to bed and tried to decide between the celestial blue chiffon nightgown and the cloudy black one with the silver stars. It was a difficult choice, but she finally decided upon the black and silver.

CHAPTER 8

He loved his role as Tancat and wanted to revel in it as long as possible. After a trip to Barcelona, he had selected the name because in Catalan it meant "closed." And that was what Communism was and should be forevermore. He knew he had been selected only because of his closeness to Paco Silva. He was aware that they doubted his leadership, at first, even his loyalty to their cause. He had convinced them, they had made the arrangements and now it was he on the scene who was in charge.

His new self-esteem had made another person of him. He felt his special limited fame was really of little importance compared with what his part could be in history. When all was over and his contribution surfaced, he was sure he would be decorated by the present government -- the government he was helping to keep in power.

Little did the others realize his role, his importance. He reveled in his sense of mystery and well being -- more so since he would soon be rid of Paco's half-baked ideas. How long had he suffered the bungling interpretations skimmed off the top of his head!

Defective theories tossed out in interviews with international writers!

This woman had at first disoriented him in spite of their assurances that she was efficient. At first glance, her looks and style had upset him. She seemed to have escaped from a Parisian fashion show or some charity ball. But what a coincidence -- she was sitting for Paco. What luck that he had seen something there he wished to paint. Now she had every opportunity. She could act at any moment. Meanwhile what fun for him to remain anonymous. In his first encounter with real international intrigue, he wanted to savor it -- to keep it all to himself as long as possible -- to be the invisible powerful manipulator behind the scenes. In short, he felt the God-like stance well suited him.

Further down the road, Miss Bennett was seated in her bedroom facing the open doors of the balcony. She held a stunning object, practically a work of art. It resembled a sparkling toy, but it was real. Especially fashioned in Florence, the first artisan with great effort had made the 22 smaller than usual. The second artisan, after firmly declaring that he was a goldsmith who could prove direct lineage from Cellini, and had never in his life worked on base metals, was gently persuaded to take the job she wanted. Yes, he would set the sapphires, but it ran against the grain. Besides it would be expensive. "What's money?" she shrugged, "only a means to have what one wants and needs." She had drawn several bills from her purse and regarded them speculatively.

"Well, I did hear that only once, after he had finished a sculpture, he worked on a silver bracelet for my lady ancestor," he conceded, "but of course, that was silver." He allowed himself to be persuaded to accept the money, and to match her spirit, did not deign to count it. He reflected that the job could be a challenge. When later he warmed to his work, he realized he too had created a work of art. It was now an exquisite piece which he kept an extra day to show to some members of his jeweler's guild.

Now as she gently and lovingly polished the stones with chamois, she thought fleetingly of him. Then she carefully loaded, engaged the safety and slipped it into her shoulder bag. It would take special planning to eliminate Benton and to take care of the

Maestro -- the main job. She thought of her fee. This would be a double liquidation and on her next New York call, she would explain the necessity and expect an adjustment in her honorarium.

She descended to the living room to telephone Benton, as she wanted to keep near him until she encountered the right moment. When she got through to him, the greetings were guarded until she suggested that they meet again to exchange more ideas on the same subject previously discussed.

"I know a great restaurant on the old Cuernavaca

Road," she told him. "Would you be free tonight or tomorrow?"

"Tomorrow will be fine," he replied. "Pick you up around seven?"

"Perfect," she answered. "Until then." She hung up smiling, and hoped this would be the start of a closer relationship, giving her better opportunities for the hit.

Benton also hung up with a smile. It was to his advantage to remain as close as possible to her. His report from New York was incomplete at the moment. Only the emergency number given her had been located and was being, of course, constantly monitored to get the lead to her employer. The investigation of "Mrs. Duran" he imagined would take longer. Considering that his immediate assignment was to protect Paco Silva, he wondered at finding himself so determined to get to the core of this woman and her employers. Surely this could be handled by others. With one call he could pass it along to another branch of his own agency. Firmly pushing this into the background, he told himself that there was certainly nothing personal in his interest, for he had deliberately hardened himself throughout the years he had been on the job, and such luxuries were not permitted in his work which now was his world. What tatters of his remaining illusions had disappeared with the breakup of the marriage he had had the naiveté to think he could maintain in his line of work.

The Gold Coin Restaurant group meeting was subdued on this evening. Don, the bartender, noted it at once and surmised that all was not as smoothly running as at their last meeting. Anthony seemed to be the center of the discussion.

"I can't imagine why, " he was saying. "Not even a confidential employee – only good for monitoring the emergency phones -- disappeared completely! Without a word. Not a trace."

"Defected?" John laughed but rather hollowly.

They all joined in, but below the surface each felt a nagging fear of the disappearance. Could it be a pickup? Although the man knew little of the various coils of the inner circle, still the thing could be damaging. Of course nothing could be proven against him, but a lead is a lead and in some way it could damage the family syndicate.

"Of course I'll have to change the communication and change the monitor," Anthony continued, noting the charged atmosphere.

They all gave marked attention to the excellent food. One or two jokes drew hearty laughter -- a shade too hearty.

"The job's become important," Anthony pursued his theme. "There's a million riding on the pictures -- we'll get that back -- she's to do the buying. A good investment if we want it. I know a guy who can black market that sort of thing. He'll buy us out there.

Then there's her pay and then our fee to the principal -- all that to be taken care of."

"You've made the arrangements so far," George commented, "Keep it up. Too many cooks spoil the cake or broth or whatever. Just do the best you can."

"Maybe it's not serious," his father smoothed it over. "Just change things around like you said and forget the missing link."

"Any phones tapped?" came the question. "Pay phone up here in New York? Impossible," Anthony replied. "The emergency phones are always changed regularly. But down there -- who knows? Who would want to?"

CHAPTER 9

Beyond a certain initial wariness, there seemed to be no sense of strain between them. During the drive to the outlying restaurant, they picked their way through inconsequential topics, incidentally finding more in common besides their love of music. As they drove along, it seemed that by common consent they had decided to save the serious matters for later. She made no effort to probe or maneuver for information and he kept to neutral subjects which seemed to flow along naturally. The cassette of Horowitz, which played, also helped with the breezy Chopin mazurkas hovering between them. Another dimension was building and both were aware of it.

The externals seemed deliberately to blend. The open car faced an incredibly full golden moon rising; the soft wind of the ride caressed their faces, floating on through the moving leaves of the trees lining the walk to the entrance of the restaurant from which the soft insistent beat of the orchestra came.

"It seems a shame to go inside and leave all this," he said taking her arm. "What a moon!"

"Ah, but we can have our cake and eat it too," she murmured. She had known this place on one of her previous visits and knew it well.

They were led up to a mezzanine completely open on one side where their table had been reserved. Muted lights alternated with the decorative live foliage surrounded by occasional fountains.

"Where are we? Inside or outside, upstairs or downstairs?" he laughed, "It's fantastic, and we've still got our moon."

"I thought you'd like it," she smiled. "And don't forget the orchestra," she indicated the half-hidden group behind some bamboo plants. "They're playing Gershwin."

"Oh God -- to think I've been here all this time and didn't know about all this!"

"I gather you're into popular music too since you did justice to your musical."

"I certainly am into it. You ought to hear my collection. I'm almost an authority on jazz and show tunes. Kurt Weill, for instance -- got almost all his stuff."

She looked up from the menu the waiter had brought. "Do you have a copy of the original version of "The Happy End?" she asked.

"That's the only thing of his I'm still missing. Hard to find."

"I have a copy -- picked up in Germany -- the folio," she said offhandedly as though two years had not been spent in locating it.

He looked at her unbelievingly, conflicting emotions rising which he now found difficult to camouflage. How was it that this woman, svelte and soignée, this hit woman, this murderess-for-pay -- how could she be a collector of his sacred Kurt Weill. And for that matter, how could she be practically a concert pianist, playing that scherzo that way?

Even now he was sure there was that little twenty-two in her sequined evening bag -- that gem-studded weapon she had probably used many times before and planned, no doubt, to use on him at the end of the evening. He had, of course, searched for and found it during one of her sitting sessions with Paco Silva. The trouble it had taken him to get the blanks for that size gun almost matched the trouble it had taken him to convince Pepe and Maria to go on his payroll.

"I'll be glad to make a copy for you. I'll send it from New York," she continued, noticing his amazement.

"Wonderful," he managed to say. And as if some devilish magic were in force, the orchestra began a Weill medley. He swallowed his wonder and decided, in for a penny, in for a pound, silently drawing her up to the small dance floor where other couples had preceded them. Minutes later he told himself that he should have known she would be the best dancer he had ever known, and, of course, it had to be the music of Kurt Weill playing. What black magic was working against him? It hardly seemed fair. It just didn't balance out. It just did not <u>scan</u>!

As she was guided through the familiar melodies, she gave a nod of approval to the captain and the orchestra leader who had both beautifully followed her instructions. These had been deliberately geared to creating the perfect evening, aimed at lowering his guard, thus permitting her more easily to keep the advantage she needed. This she felt she had so far retained, that he was the mouse to her cat. Yet as the music slid into "Speak Low" and they glided effortlessly until the end, she began to wonder if her own machinations were ricocheting. She had to remind herself that this was to be one of the exploratory projects designed to gauge the subject carefully with the view of facilitating the best time and manner of liquidation.

Later as they were served, he regarded the various dishes attractively garnished and knew the food would also be superb. Again he wished the whole charade could be for real, and not for the first time pondered his choice of profession thinking cynically of the philosophy of his Washington bureau and its demands.

When much later the pause came which both recognized as the serious part of the evening, he took the initiative.

"I know you invited me here to talk about the general situation concerning Paco Silva and your safety," he began, looking directly into her eyes, "but I have a very good idea about that."

"I'm listening," she smiled almost sure of what he would say.

"Well, for me so far it's a terrific evening. You know, perhaps, that to live in a foreign country makes one miss a lot of things -- for instance; we seldom hear these songs they're playing. In short -- since the evening is so special, let's just finish it out as it is. We can talk another time."

"Play it as it lays?" she laughed. "I was going to suggest the same thing."

"Let's dance again," he suggested, rising...and if she kills me tonight, he thought, what a way to go!

It was two-thirty as he headed for his place after seeing her home.

Right up to the end, the time had spun out in the same dream-like magic. There had been more dancing, more talk, another round of liqueurs, and finally the drive to her house to the sound of Paco Lucia's classical guitar on his car's stereo. Pepe had been waiting to open the gate, smiling as usual, making Miss Bennett quite sure that he approved of a romance he suspected.

Now as Benton rounded the curve of his own driveway, he was surprised to see a Chevrolet with Mexican tags in front of his door. He was sure his houseman whom he had prohibited to stay up for him, had not admitted any stranger. Entering, he was happy to see it was Clem Spencer, a friend and colleague with whom he had worked several times in Europe. He found him slouched in an armchair with a drink listening to some early New Orleans jazz on the stereo.

"My God! What brings you here?" he exclaimed after some back slapping and firm handshakes.

"Never mind that. Where the hell have you been all night?" was the reply. Clem, tall and slim, usually reserved, ugly in such a special way that he could pass for good looking, was around forty. His manner suggested a dependable favorite uncle who was sure to select the right Christmas presents and never forget one's birthday.

"No fair holding back. Don't start playing cute and drive me nuts," Benton admonished, getting himself a cognac. "Tell me right off -- you're not on vacation. They've sent you down to work with me! Straight from Washington -- technically Virginia, that is."

"Right." Clem resumed his seat after lowering the music. "Lots to tell you. But how's it going? They filled me in somewhat up there -- read all your reports. Any more input? Tune me in."

"Complications as usual, but different. I'm glad you came so I can talk it out." He proceeded to outline his problems protecting the great Paco Silva; his stubbornness, the communicating difficulties, above all, his ego rejecting any thought of danger. Then in detail he spoke of his luck in discovering the source of the hit. He described Miss Bennett.

"I was with her tonight," he continued. "She invited me to this fabulous place -- terrific food, drink and music. All set up, of course, to lull me away from any suspicions I might have -- to cast a spell -- to enchant -- and I regret to tell you, she almost did. But more than that -- I do not trust the woman -- she's capable of anything -- anything standing in her way. And that could include me!"

"Hmmm."

"And I don't even know her first name. She calls herself Mrs. Duran, but you can imagine how legitimate that is."

"Sexy?"

"Not the way you mean. Not the least. In the first place, she's either in her late twenties or early thirties -- hard to tell these days. Then she's not all that pretty. But she's got something..."

"je ne sais quoi?"

"Exactly."

"Snazzy dresser?"

"Exquisite. Looks like it's Paris or Italy. But tonight she wore a embroidered cotton -- you know, what they do here -- looks like a print, -- you remember our in-training fabric class."

"Yep -- almost died of boredom."

"Now I almost believe in those names they give those perfumes! Hers tonight had to be named Dangerous -- or just plain Danger!"

"Hmmm."

"But what I don't understand is her background. She's a concert-caliber pianist -- I know 'cause it's my hobby. How the hell does she figure as a hit woman?"

"Like I say, stranger things have happened."

"And not only might she shoot me, but she's sitting for a portrait daily with Paco Silva!"

"God a'mighty!" Clem smiled and stretched his long legs out further.

"You're pretty cool tonight!" Benton rose, circled his chair and selected another. "And would you mind telling me if you're holding back? What's the mumbo-jumbo at headquarters? What about my lead into the New York telephone number?"

Clem ran his fingers through his early-graying hair and pulled a large brown envelope from his breast coat pocket.

"We're moving along, Pal, but remember it was just that one number to go on -- can't work miracles."

"I know all about miracles or lack of same."

"Also we've combed every commuter-distance New Jersey town -- Julliard grad -- tough boring assignment. But we did it. Found the lady we think. Here's your report -- detailed." He threw it over to Benton who caught it and tore it open, grumbling something about unwarranted delay.

The following silence was broken only when Clem moved to select another tape, and shortly a Fletcher Henderson arrangement for Benny Goodman played.

Benton groaned as he turned the pages. Minutes passed with only the sound of music. Finally lowering the report, Benton walked over to the bar and poured himself a double cognac, forgetting to check Clem's glass. He resumed his chair, picked up the report and slapped it.

"Lots of stuff here -- young couple, Gail and James Blake -- husband Captain in the Marines, killed with his company in that massacre in Iran. She begins to teach music in the Englewood schools. Young daughter raped and killed, as she takes shortcut through wooded area -- criminal never caught. Widow moves to New York -- address unknown, but keeps up the Jersey home and sometimes visits. Calls neighbors asking for daughter. They think she's crazy -- should be committed. But how in hell do we know that this Mrs. Duran is that same person? This woman has no traces of being a housewife. Far from it!" But even as he spoke an independent part of his mind was fitting several pieces in alignment. The material just read could account for the piano virtuosity of Mrs. Duran -- the diploma from Julliard. Also her cultural background and something even more significant was dawning -- the tremendous possible motive for becoming what he almost knew this Mrs. Duran to be.

"Look, Greg," the unflappable Clem drawled, "you asked for us to locate the background of a certain person -- living in a commutable New Jersey town, female music teacher, age about thirty, graduate of Julliard School of Music. We did it. Now it's up to you to establish the link -- if it does exist."

"Yes, I know -- and don't think I don't appreciate the fast work you did, a great report," He paused to collect his thoughts. "I haven't mentioned my Embassy contact. By the way, I gather you've done a recent check on my house here and my telephone. I check it daily -- but don't know about tonight. Can we really talk?"

"Yes. Checked on all that while I waited. Your houseman wasn't too enthused -- good thing he knew me from before."

"My cover's still O.K.," Benton told him. "No electronic devices here up to now. But I'm vigilant. By the way, I'm a leading light on the amateur acting group here, and I write magazine articles."

There followed explanations, changes of strategy, new strategy, all far into the morning, leaving Benton with a sense of well being, having now the invaluable help of an old ally. He knew now that he had needed support without realizing it.

It was almost dawn when Clem drove off in his rented car to his hotel, and Benton headed for his well-earned bed.

CHAPTER 10

"It's going splendidly," Paco told his coterie on his coffee break. "That means a long break today. Pierre, I want you to see how it's shaping up."

This departure from his usual custom was noted at once. Cecile scribbled busily and rose to snap the group with her ever-ready camera. At these moments, they would all in some subtle manner turn toward the camera, to assure their inclusion in the photo.

"Any time, Paco, just say the word," Pierre replied.

"God, what a day -- and to think it's still March," Paco exclaimed stretching out arms and legs as he leaned back and observed the cloudless

blue sky.

"It's snowing hard in Paris," Jeanne commented. "I just heard the news on TV."

"And even on the Riviera, there's some snow," Michele added not to be outdone.

"And that helps us to enjoy this weather all the more," Pelayo said as he approached the table for coffee.

"And where is Mrs. Duran?" inquired Henry Parks blinking through his thick horn rims.

"Oh, she's in there. And today I turned my work to the wall. Don't trust her not to look at it since it's almost finished."

"You've only been a month on it," ventured Jeanne, knowing this could be a delicate area.

But Paco was in an expansive mood. "Yes, only a month, but guess what? I'm almost finished. Maybe only another month at the most -- maybe."

It was as though a bombshell had dropped. They exclaimed at this, having guessed that it was developing into an important work and remembering that some of his works had taken many months and sometimes years to finish.

A ring at the garden gate came, and shortly Antonio Munillo entered followed by his sword boy carrying his capes and swords. Few of his fans would have recognized him, fresh from his daily training with jogging suit hanging limply on his slim muscular body. He blotted his strong features wreathed in a wide smile using a large red-printed cotton handkerchief and pushed his wet hair from his eyes.

"Please excuse me," he begged. "Hate to join you like this, but I'm starved. I had to pass by here, and couldn't wait to change!" He flopped into the chair his sword boy pulled over.

He was cordially greeted in the manner always used with one of the in-group -- one of their own. Furthermore, he was scheduled to fight in Plaza Mexico on the following Sunday as the star attraction. Jeanne anticipated Michele in springing up to order breakfast for him.

"And an American breakfast," he called after her, "not continental." He turned toward them and complained. "Scarcely anybody knows what we go through -- bullfighters - - matadors -- I get so sick of those movies where the matador is always seen with ten or twenty pretty girls -- always sitting in nightclubs and all that wine, women and song. They never speak about how we have to train every single day -- live like monks when we're fighting -- worry about the kind of bulls we get -- how the public will receive us -- all that grief: Sometimes the bull is the least we have to fight, damn it! Got to fight politics too, the lordly impresarios and their friends -- not to mention the competition -- Oh Lord!" He waxed eloquent as his audience seemed flatteringly attentive. "Now I am expected to hold up the honor of Spain when I'm fighting in Plaza Mexico next Sunday. If one of those Mexican matadors comes across better than my fight, they will whistle and shout nasty things about my work -- maybe a couple of loud voices will announce the time the Spanish-Line plane leaves for Spain. This happened to me once!"

"And if you triumph?" asked Henry Parks.

"I must be fair. If I triumph, the crowd will give me credit. I can't deny the Mexican aficionados aren't fair. I've won several ears in that plaza and some tails too."

"Ears?" Michele repeated.

"Oh do hide your ignorance," Paco chided. "By now you should know when a matador does his work well, he is awarded the ear of the animal and shows it as he walks around the arena, to the roars of the crowd."

"And if he does very well," Pierre added, "he gets two ears."

"And the tail of the animal if he does a phenomenal job." Paco resumed. "We must go to see Antonio Sunday. I will make sketches there from life."

"Oh I appreciate that, Maestro," Antonio answered. "You are always so kind to me, you do me honor. Let's pray I don't get another goring. I'm really tired of being on the oilcloth!"

"I try to tell these feather heads about all that," Paco feelingly explained, "but it goes in one ear and comes out the other. All they see is that smashing suit of lights -- all those sequins -- the smooth pass of the bull who could turn any moment to kill you. They yell Olé and drink wine from the wineskins, buy their pistachio nuts and wait for the next bull. The majority don't even know what it's all about!"

"Right," agreed Antonio between gulps of coffee.

Cecile rose to snap Antonio as he ate, including Paco, of course, who was looking on approvingly. One never knew what the editors would most like, and she was going to be prepared to have plenty of material from which they could choose.

Meanwhile, inside the studio, Miss Bennett continued her pacing which so rested her muscles. She carried her coffee cup, sipping as she went. The half hour of waiting alone was not as boring as it could have been to another more attuned to company. Yet, a saying occasionally crossed her mind. "What price glory?" She fully realized the honor bestowed upon her, but the only reason for acceding to pose for Silva was the advantage of the access to the villa and to Paco himself. But first, she reminded herself, she must deal with Gregory Benton.

She was sure she had allayed his obvious suspicion of her, with the invitation extended two weeks ago. In a strange way, she had enjoyed the evening with him, but had kept her motive in mind at all times. She must act soon, for she sensed the portrait was nearing completion and that would obviate the ready access. Furthermore, with Benton out of the way, the following Sunday could see the demise of Silva what with the golden opportunity of the bullfight in nearby Mexico City.

The entrance of Silva and Pierre interrupted her thinking and she patiently waited until Pierre had seen and evaluated the portrait; she noted his enthusiasm. When he left, she silently resumed her pose.

As usual, night fell softly. The sunset was spectacular, mingling gold with the soft mauves and pinks, all fading slowly into a memorable afterglow. Dusk sidled in gently with an enormous rising moon -- the problem. The poetic moonlight shedding radiance over the landscape, bathing the world in lambent splendor made her angry. She needed a darker night to feel comfortable for the task before her. Even later as she watched the smaller midnight moon rising higher, she still preferred less light. She would have to risk it, for time was running out fast. This was not the rainy season and it would be months before she could hope for an overcast sky.

She dressed in black slacks and shirt and changed to dark running shoes with heavy rubber soles. At the mirror she tucked her hair under a black beret. Looking out into the garden she saw no lights in the gatehouse. Now she had free egress without the too- accommodating Pepe and Maria to offer help. What would they think of her excursion at that hour in the clothes she now wore? They would insist upon accompanying her. Impossible!

Fitting her twenty-two into the deep pocket of her slacks left both hands completely free. Without lights, she made her way downstairs and slowly opened the enormous carved- wood front door. Suddenly she felt Emily brush against her ankles. With a sigh of annoyance she gently pushed her back into the house, pulled the door shut after adjusting the heavy lock for her reentry.

She walked at the edge of the soft flowerbeds, skirting away from the gatehouse until she came to the high wall surrounding the property. The vines covering it were strong with years of growth. As she tested them, only a few tendrils pulled away with her weight. Grasping a handful of the tough foliage, she got traction with the rubber soles as they met the rough stonewall beneath the vines. Gradually she climbed, inching her way to the top without too much rustling. She hoped the wind in the trees, the whirring wings of the occasional night bird could cover whatever sound her climb made. She reached the top and found the descent easier. At last on firm ground, she dusted herself, inspected her hands and was glad to find her fingernails intact. She realized she should have worn gloves.

The street seemed deserted, but she knew she was likely to encounter some kind of late night stroller at any time. She squared her shoulders, began to whistle a Mexican song and with a slight swagger, sauntered up the cobblestone street, sure that she could find Gregory Benton's house on foot. By car it had seemed quite close, but in the dimly lit streets, some unpaved, others deserted, the distance took on a new dimension. She hurried a bit and crossed the street as she neared a house disgorging guests from a party.

Several cars passed her and slowed, as if trying to identify her as a boy or girl. At this hour of night, she knew there would be trouble should it be decided she was a woman, for no women who were "good" would dare be out alone at this hour in either town or country.

She turned the corner and recognized a street she thought led to Benton's place, but crowning her fears, two weaving figures appeared approaching. They were supporting and encouraging each other. She sauntered to the other side of the street, but one of them called out.

"Joven! Hey you, young man! Come over here and have a drink. Tequila, very good too! Good tequila!"

"Thanks. Another time!! She answered gruffly and continued walking. But the man raised his voice and demanded, "Think you're too good to drink with us, right? Think you're too good! Know what you are? A junior. That's what you are -- a señorito -- spoiled rich brat! I hate rich people. Think they're so much!" Then began between the two men a tirade against every snub encountered since childhood. They lamented their fate for having been born poor. Then they loudly finished up by describing what they would someday do to all the rich people they would meet in the future. In complete agreement, they crossed the street and began to follow her shouting the litany.

She knew what she had to do. Swagger exaggerated, she turned around and approached them making the sign for silence. "Where's the bottle?" she loudly whispered. "It's my papa! I sneaked from the house. Do not betray me!"

These words in Spanish carried weight and her brusque snatch of the offered bottle underlined it. "Got to know about life sometime," she muttered.

"That's the spirit," one of them approved after his initial surprise.

Firmly clasping the bottle and telling herself that alcohol kills germs, she drank almost an ounce. "Ah," she smiled, rubbing her stomach. "Thanks. Not to be impolite and greedy, but can I have another bit?" Strangely enough the tequila had "fallen well" upon the stomach, to translate a common Spanish idiom. It helped her maintain her facade and seemed to prepare her for her future nocturnal project. I needed that! She almost laughed to herself. Had she but known, the liquor was not tequila at all, but a stronger brew known as Mesqual.

"After me -- my turn," the first man said, reaching for the bottle, now a little worried about the quantity left. "Look here, we're bricklayers -- finished this afternoon with that building down the street. The jefe gave us a party -- and with mariachis too!"

"It's the custom," she said.

"Yes, the custom," he nodded sagely and tottered a bit.

"Let's sit down here," she suggested. "More comfortable."

As they were still weaving, they were quick to follow her example on the high irregular curbstone. They passed the bottle fairly among them, and she took her turn with it.

"Now I never thought of sitting down," the second bricklayer confided. "See how smart some of these juniors are -- very intelligent."

They were silent a moment until the first worker politely rose turning his back to urinate against the nearby fence. Returning, he explained, "Excuse me but I had to "un- water' myself."

They excused him, both nodding their understanding of the problem. Five minutes passed and the two men began to hum a popular song, later singing out the words happily. Their voices harmonized beautifully, but Miss Bennett did not doubt that a "Señor policia" could not fail to come along shortly led by the ongoing duet and perhaps anticipating a "bite" -- a little tip for not arresting them for intoxication.

She jumped up suddenly. "Oh my God! Look over there! Help me -- here comes my Papa!"

Nobody was coming, but she guessed that the power of suggestion would be strong in their condition. Also it would take some time for them to struggle to their feet in case they decided to follow her. She pointed slightly behind them and began to run, hearing but faintly their comments on how wealthy people never knew how to raise their children -- keeping them sheltered when they should learn about <u>life</u>.

The incident as well as the alcohol had sharpened her senses. She felt alive and stimulated, more aware of her ultimate purpose. She began to anticipate it. Except for two more passing cars, the rest of the walk was uneventful. She turned into Benton's street and was relieved to see there were no lights visible from the top of the surrounding wall. Belatedly she thought of Pedro -- did he sleep in or come in as a daily? Lack of time had denied her the set up.

Scaling the wall was easier than that of her own house, and by now she had acquired more skill. A soft jump found her inside the patio. She crept around to the side looking for a likely window -- one perhaps already open. If not, the small glass cutter in her other pocket would help with the same technique Benton had used earlier in her house.

She approached a promising glass door, not without having to crush some flowers in the bed approaching the brick steps leading to it. Gently she began her work, glad now for the moonlight which she had previously deplored. In minutes she entered and identified the room even in the half-gloom as the large living room. She then thought of his car and carefully retraced her steps to check the carport on the other side of the house, trying to avoid the scurrying chameleons in the pathway and several other night creatures, which she preferred not to examine too closely. The car was there. Careful! Careful! She made her way back and again entered the room, adjusting her vision to the pale moonlight filtering through the windows.

"I've been waiting for you, Gail!" came the voice as lights flooded the place from all sides.

She whirled around, and saw Benton seated in one of the large leather chairs, dressed in jeans and shirt. Even in the shock of her surprise she noticed the revolver on the table beside him, watched as he lifted it.

"Come in, Gail," he invited before she could speak, "but don't reach in your pocket whatever you do."

She stood and stared at him. Of all the conflicting emotions now surging, anger at his advantage and her vulnerability dominated. It was the first time she had met the situation.

"Sit over here, Gail," he directed indicating a chair on the other side of his table.

"My name is Heather," she replied stepping forward. She removed her beret, shook out her hair and unhurriedly sat in the indicated chair.

He carefully offered her a cigarette which she refused. She was chagrined to find on the table a chilled daiquiri which seemed to have been waiting for her. The proof.

"I made it as soon as I got the signal you were climbing my back gate," he said noticing her glance at the glass.

"Thank you," she answered and proceeded to sip it. "I just finished a cocktail on the curbstone near here with some friends, but I don't mind mixing drinks. I could use this. Very thoughtful."

He too seemed in no hurry. "Thought you'd need it." His face now was the one she had seen in the mirror while playing his piano -- how long had it been, she wondered. How a difference in an expression could make a person. Gone was the man she had danced with, the man who sang so well. She silently regarded him as she sipped. There was nothing for her to say, so she remained silent.

"Did you by any chance think the place would be unguarded?" he asked. "All the windows were unlocked -- that business with the glass cutter was so unnecessary. Thought you'd never get here."

"Really?"

"Yes, really. Perhaps you'd like to explain."

She finished the cocktail and lowered the glass deliberately. Then matching his stare, she pointed an accusing finger at him. "Come off it! Did you or did you not enter my house the same way?"

"I did. But I was checking it out. That's my work!" Not expecting this gambit he felt a rising anger at being put on the defensive under the circumstances.

"That's exactly what I was doing too, and that's my work also."

"Your work? Tell me more about your work, Gail Blake!"

"Tell me about yours. You say you're a detective. So am I."

He gave a derisive laugh. The use of her real name and the laugh told her everything, including the tapping of her telephone which she now guessed. Why had she ever mentioned the State of New Jersey to him? Yet, now knowing him for more than just a local bodyguard, she used a defense she had perfected by enveloping herself in an invisible protective armour. Her eyes, though still meeting his, became impenetrable showing neither fear nor alarm.

"My name is Heather Duran," she said.

He was the first to look away as his previous doubt surfaced.

Was Gail Blake the same woman as Heather Duran? Yet that telephone conversation ... still holding his gun in the other hand. "Would you like another?"

"Why not? Then I'll be leaving," she said.

Silently, continually facing her, he placed his gun before him on the bar.

She watched slightly amused at his precaution. Using both hands he mixed ingredients and shook the mixture.

"If you ever retire from detecting, you'd make a great bartender," she said. Later with the new drink over the first, plus the raw mescal she had taken, she felt a welcoming warmth, just enough to give her the perspective she needed.

"Perhaps you'd like some music," he said ironically, to counter her seeming well being which he failed to understand.

"Why not?"

He backed to the control nearby and, compounding the irony floating between them, the strains of "Speak Low" flooded the room. He had forgotten he had been playing music earlier. Involuntarily their eyes met for a second and the memory of their last evening flashed. She listened silently as he resumed his chair still armed. When the song ended she finished her drink and rose.

"I really must go," she said as though leaving from a social call.

Nettled at her <u>sang froid</u>, he also rose, and for a moment they stood where they were as the song went into another arrangement. He placed the gun on a table and approached her.

To her surprise and his own, he took her in his arms and began to move to the music. She had little choice but to follow as his tense body and hands sent a message. This was no ordinary dance. He was holding her close and his face had not changed.

Gradually his hand closed tightly on her wrist, and still in time to the music, now uncomfortably close, hurting her back and shoulders, he put his lips to her ear and whispered, "If anything happens to Paco Silva, I am going to kill you!"

Embraced in a grip of iron, she would have died rather than complain at the increasing discomfort which she knew was inflicted because of his frustration and apparent inability to get to her. She said nothing. The song ended, and he abruptly released her, took up his gun, hustled her without a word through another door to the carport, into the car, and drove off to her house with the silence heavy between them.

At the gate he got out and rang for Pepe who sleepily answered after a few minutes, giving expressions of surprise and concern that she had been out of the house. Neither said goodbye.

Explaining nothing to Pepe, she went upstairs and began another discipline to discard everything from thought except the business of the moment -- sleep. She undressed, selected another favorite gown -- the frosty beige silk, hand-embroidered with margaritas. Her sheets had already been folded back and the down pillows fluffed. After carefully cold creaming her face and bathing her slightly scuffed hands in a rich lotion, she sank gratefully into bed. The only disturbing factor marring the practice discipline was the song clearly continuing to play in her brain -- "Speak Low."

"Damn it," she said aloud.

"Well, what do you think?" Benton asked as he returned.

"Cool customer, Clem answered. "But I had you covered the whole time from the coat closet -- all that gun play you were doing, Ha!"

"I know. But even with that, and the blanks in the piece of jewelry she carries around I didn't trust my luck. She's a pro, you know. Might have even spotted the blanks."

"Never saw you like that -- even dancing with her: What the hell goes on?"

Benton flushed and went over to the bar, scooped up some ice and poured. "How the hell do I know? I play everything by ear. I have to -- but you couldn't hear what I told her while doing the light fantastic. I told her I would kill her if anything happened to Silva."

"Well, well, well," Clem answered eyeing him narrowly. "Do tell!"

"Do tell indeed," Benton replied, gulping his drink. "And some day you'll get tired of imitating that Western hero you saw in the movies when you were ten years old."

"Well now, I mought, and then again I moughtent," Clem answered, smiling maddeningly.

CHAPTER 11

An uneventful month passed. There had been no more contact with Gregory Benton, yet she felt a surveillance, of person and of house. There seemed too many workmen fixing the street in front of the villa. There were also peddlers ringing the bell at the gate, and even Maria and Pepe seemed always underfoot.

The subtle difference in her mental state disturbed and surprised her. To her dismay, flashes of the "why" of her assignment crept in unbidden -- dismay because she had never wanted or allowed any knowledge of motives to mar any of her assignments. Meanwhile she tried to reject the intruding figure of Benton during these reflections, wanting to dispose of him literally and figuratively at the earliest moment in spite of her strong suspicion of his government connection.

All of this she mentally tossed around with the astounding knowledge that her emergency telephone in New York had failed for the first time. There had been no answer to her ring at whatever anonymous corner of New York she had called. And all the while faithfully sitting daily for Silva as she had promised. She pondered her future moves, always remembering the direct threat Benton had given her while dancing.

She now watched Silva concentrating on his canvas, glancing frequently at her, still humming first louder then softer to the music, still with his Beatles and his beloved Bach. She wanted to hate him, to move away from her emotionless reaction to him and his sycophants. She tried to remember that book written by a former mistress with its references to his parsimony, to the fact that his concurrent mistresses had to be always available. It seemed they were always present in tandem -- a matter of frequent reference by him to his friends. Her thoughts wandered to his present protégée, and the other girl whom she had heard referred to as his "social" secretary, to distinguish her from Pelayo's title. Mistresses both, and living in the same house, this fact never marring the adulation of the "toadys" who thought he could do no wrong. She thought of the arrogant manner in which he treated one and all and the same arrogance with which he treated her -- as any hired model.

"Please!" Paco stood in front of her, hands on hips of his now frayed blue shorts looking at her strangely. "What has happened to you? Your face has changed!"

She was struck that he was aware of the difference in her thinking though she had thought she had maintained her exact expression. "Just a little tired, Maestro," she excused herself. "I have a feeling it's time for my break. I need some coffee about now."

"Take fifteen minutes," he grandly conceded. "I'll have mine too -- outside -- no peeking now -- I'm going to let you see it at the end of this session. I'm almost finished."

A chill ran over her. Though she had known this day would come, still it surprised her. Thank goodness for the still-to-be bought pictures. She recovered and attempted a smile, but he had turned and without further comment had padded out into the garden. Within minutes a maid came in with the usual tray of thin sandwiches and today some petit fours, and the needed coffee. She ate while pacing as usual, never once having been tempted to have a look at the painting, being devoid of curiosity about it. She now wanted only to be rid of this chore of which everyone felt she should feel so honored.

For several days Tancat had been figuratively sulking in his tent. Action was what he had expected sooner, and there was that bitch arriving every day to sit for Paco and not doing a damned thing to eliminate him. Then too there had been no answer to that New York emergency telephone number that he had repeatedly tried, in order to bolster his assurance. Recently everything seemed to have gone wrong. His contact would be getting impatient and if things continued thus, he would lose his newly achieved prestige. There might be a transfer of power. And just when everything was going so well previously. "I hate women!" he intoned every night in bed. "I could kill her, the bitch!" Maybe he really could some day. In his methodical way he contemplated several methods, such as boiling in oil, depositing her on a desert island to starve to death and hanging her from the highest tree in Cuernavaca, and there were some pretty high ones available too. Meanwhile, along the same lines, why couldn't he do the job on Paco himself? He had the opportunity -- access to the villa at all times, and who could believe he had done the deed -- allied as he had been for so many years as one of Silva's pets. He began to run these thoughts around as if trying them on for size.

As he now sat, listening to Paco airing his half-baked polemics almost daring anyone to disagree with him, he inwardly writhed in his annoyance. With two sentences, he couldn't help demolishing Paco's premise to the surprise of everyone. He just could not help it. They all looked inquiringly at him, Paco glaring balefully. Well, might as well go for broke, thought Tancat as he added insult to injury by saying, "Paco, you really should stick more to art. Your old theory of Communism could never work in real life. Look what has happened to it -- that's proof enough. The one or two countries left will have to eliminate it eventually. We experts know that and so do they!"

A shocked silence followed.

"You seem to know it all," Paco exploded throwing up his hands. "Suppose you just tell us your own views of the perfect society without stealing your ideas from all those people you're forever quoting."

Tancat subsided after flinching at that direct insult. Although remaining silent, it was at that moment he decided on his plan to do the job himself.

It would be like therapy for him to do it. Oh, the satisfaction to relieve himself of all built-up frustrations, of all the humiliating throw-offs not only insulting his superior knowledge, but his personal dignity. All had been fine and they had been good friends until the recent turnover with the disappearance of Communism. It would be so different if Silva knew -- really knew -- anything about politics, but in his effort to occupy all areas of knowledge, including politics and art, everybody in the world had to listen and conform to his views. It was insupportable! And it justified his resolve. He would do the job, and the world would certainly be a better place. And some day when his heroic deed became known to everyone, he would be hailed as the hero he was, cutting away the poison that Paco was still disseminating. Paco returned to the studio with a springy step, contented that he had demolished the criticism of his ex-disciple, for he planned to forbid him to his group after humiliating him further in front of the others. He was now beyond the pale, a state Paco had created, meaning something similar to outer space banishment, nonexistence. He had had a hint of rebellion before from that same party. And now he had the direct proof -- and his nerve in telling him to "stick to art!" His hackles rose as he sat before his painting and paused a few moments to adjust his thinking.

As he sat, all past annoyances faded as the strength and mastery of his work almost overwhelmed him. An artist works hard on every project, but something inside, somewhere inside, urges the mind and body to recognize when a masterpiece has arrived. This had happened now. He gloated for a while, filled with a sense of wonder and completion at his own genius. He knew now his egotism was unnecessary for genius often took over and occupied all inner and out space for him.

"At first you interested me with your good bones," he spoke as though talking to himself, "but then there came something else, something that demanded more and more. I had no idea I would spend so much time on it. I'm surprised at the result. I might just keep it for my own private collection."

She murmured appropriate responses never shifting her pose.

"I know when I've put in the power of my art," he continued. "I know. And the critics will know too -- not that I care about them -- but the public will know -- even the public!"

She was quiet as he seemed to be adding touches -- she hoped the finishing touches. He worked for a long while, longer than usual, even giving her two more rest breaks. Lunch hour came and went, and since she was assured that this was the last sitting, she did not remind him of it. A discreet knock on the studio door had been ignored, and nobody dared insist.

"Of course, I have yet to put my special sealer," he finally announced stepping back from the canvas, but now you may look at this painting I have achieved. I know it is good, but see what you think with your real face looking at the ones I painted. I want to experience that!"

She rose stretching almost cramped muscles. "Now? I can look?" she spoke as if to remind him of the earlier prohibition.

"Yes, now," he answered unaware, and rested his brushes on his palette with great care.

She stepped down and crossed to the canvas prepared to see an enlarged oil of the working sketch he had previously shown her. Later she remembered very little of what followed. She stood before the canvas, and as Silva watched, she took her first and last look at what was later to be considered one of the foremost masterpieces of Francisco Silva.

It had nothing to do with the original sketch. She had been sincere when she had told him he possessed the insight of the gods, but she had not then been aware of the profundity of this insight. His impressionism had always been based upon a solid technical foundation as much of his earlier works in various important museums attested. And this, fused with his unerring eye which probed to the core of his subject had yielded the result she now beheld.

What she saw in the three-quarter life-sized canvas was her present face with a strange arresting quality which held attention. But then gradually there appeared the other face. How he had done it would remain his own technique never to be copied. After studying the first face, the other face emerged, and that other was a faithful replica of herself as she had been ten years ago. It was exactly the face she had seen in her wedding picture. And that face also held the viewer. It cast a spell difficult to explain. To her, it was compelling, seeming to foretell all that was to happen to her.

She stood immobile for a long while and he watched her, enchanted with her reaction. As she stood there, she felt the old malady returning. The man was a seer -- he was unearthly. How could he have known her then? How could he have probed into her other self -- her other existence? As her thoughts raced along, she knew what was happening and fought it savagely, to no avail. Hitherto she had tried to induce forgetfulness at the New Jersey house, almost achieving the personality division, almost feeling that she was her former self waiting for Terry to come home. Yet that iota of normalcy had always remained. But now, as she felt the familiar oncoming split vision and nausea, to be followed by a pounding headache, she desperately feared she would experience the true division, feeling herself marching backward in time.

She swayed, and Silva, still greatly pleased, righted her and suggested she sit for a moment.

"You are surprised," he said, gratified as he delightedly scratched his stomach. "You'll see much more when it dries!"

She leaned back in the chair and shut her eyes. Silence reigned while he made a few extra touches to the edges of the portrait. Now, as she had anticipated, came the hammer-like pounding in her head, and with it came something else. It was as though she had indeed raced back to inhabit the body of her former self, as Terry's mother. What had she been doing the years in between? Here was this genius whose work she had always admired -- even bought. How depraved had she become? What had she been doing? She knew the answers even as she asked herself the questions.

Silva glanced at her, still contented with her reaction which he took as a fitting compliment, but he did a double take as he now saw the second face -- the earlier version she was now showing. Gone was the blank look of her eyes. "It is the other you!" he said wonderingly. "I knew it was there even if you did not show me!" he marveled, unknowingly sending a shaft through her, for she did indeed feel like the other.

"Leave Mexico!" she said in a choked voice he barely recognized.

He started at her, shocked.

"Leave at once!" she repeated.

"What in the world are you saying?" he demanded, wondering if she had taken leave of her senses.

She shut her eyes, aware of the problem facing her involving Paco Silva.

"You're sick," he continued. "You do not eat enough. People like you never do. You do not take your food seriously enough -- a common mistake in this hemisphere."

She almost laughed at him. His very life was threatened and he was speaking of food.

"I'm sick -- yes. Have been for years. But you can't understand that now. And there's no time to explain -- no time to waste. Do you know what the word <u>danger</u> means? It's danger -- it's your life!" she leaned forward to emphasize her warning.

"Oh, for God's sake," he scoffed, "another nut! That fellow, Benton, has been telling me a lot of cloak and dagger stuff! I'm Paco Silva! Everyone respects me!"

"You're an egomaniac fool!" she almost shouted, rising.

"How dare you!" he recoiled, greatly surprised.

"I'm trying to save your life! They've fingered you -- I don't know who! I've got the contract! Me, your lilac and silver lady. Do you understand me? I'm speaking your language, Spanish!"

Her new authority made him hesitate a moment, but he quickly recovered.

"But who could want me out of the way? Is this some joke? Why?"

"God knows," she answered, still fighting her pain and loss of peripheral vision. "It's something to do with your politics, I guess. Either change whatever it is, or go into hiding -- whichever, but leave Mexico today!"

"I'll do what I please!" he responded belligerently. "Somebody is trying to scare me from speaking out, threatening me -- but they would not dare! I don't scare easily -- I am Paco Silva -- world famous!" He thrust his head forward. "And as for you -- with your what did you say? Your 'contract'? I certainly would like to see somebody like you handle a gun! You are sent here to scare me off!"

"You'd like to see me handle a gun?" she almost laughed. "Never mind." She had resumed her seat with a new onslaught of head throbbing, but she struggled to her feet and faced him. "Nobody can talk to you. Your ego is insufferable!"

He turned on her in violent anger. "Woman, I am a genius! How dare you speak to me like this!"

"And genius is your excuse to step on people -- denigrate women -- lord knows how many..."

"You are sick! You are crazy!" he almost screamed.

"No -- I'm well now," she replied moving toward the picture. "It's all there -- you painted it all!"

"You get out of here -- get out! Never come back! I won't have it!" His face contorted, he backed nearer the canvas as though protecting it.

She sighed and walked slowly to the garden door quelling the temptation to convince him, but seeing the futility of it. As she left, she heard him shouting to someone to bring him a cognac.

Home at last, she took the tranquilizer her long-deserted psychiatrist had given her. She had not returned to his office beyond that one visit, and he had called her to predict a dire future. "It couldn't be worse than the present," she had replied. But now, she wondered. She closed the curtains of her bedroom, kept on the sunglasses and lay over the bed until she fell into a troubled sleep. Something or someone inside her was intoning -- you are still Gail Blake -- remember Gail Blake?

It was almost dark when she awakened, glad Pepe and Maria had obeyed orders not to disturb her. Uncertainly she began packing, opening the door to admit Emily who was scratching at it. Later Mariq brought up a light repast which she ate out on the balcony. She resumed packing to the consternation of the couple who wondered if they had been found to be disloyal. They regretted having capitulated to Benton, allowing him to examine her bedroom in her absence. They felt guilty and vacillated between confessing what they termed their "sin" and maintaining their guilty silence.

Meanwhile she was moving slowly into the role of Gail who seemed to be taking over, replacing Heather Bennett. It was a difficult, exhausting process, accompanied by the constant headache. The nausea had gone and she had recovered the peripheral vision, but a heavy feeling of guilt oppressed her and she postponed trying to remember the events of the past few years. Yet she could not postpone thinking of Paco Silva. How could she have possibly imagined doing harm to an artist of his caliber? She now equated him with a Beethoven or a Brahms. She had admired his work for years, even had managed to buy it at prohibitive prices. And now she had sat for him with the blackest of black plans. What had she said to him? She cringed at the surging memory.

She made plane reservations by phone, and decided to retire early to be ready for the trip in the morning to the Mexico City Airport. Taking another capsule, she selected a nightgown at random and sank into bed praying for sleep, hoping to block the crowding thoughts, recriminations, and future decisions to be made. Strangely enough, she did sleep, and soundly.

That was why she did not hear the commotion at the gatehouse around two the next morning. She heard nothing until Maria entered her room and gently touched her arm to awaken her.

"Señora, Señora," she called softly, "Please wake up -- please! They want you downstairs."

Slowly she awakened to see Maria bending over her dressed in a wrapper, a long braid hanging over her shoulder.

"Señora! Pardon this intrusion, but the Maestro and his friend insist on entering! He is almost crazy!"

"What Maestro?" she asked, not fully awake.

"That artist man -- the Maestro!"

As she sprang from bed, pulling on a robe, she heard voices raised below.

"Where is she, where is she?" Paco was demanding of a still protesting Pepe. "I demand asylum! Where is she?"

"I'm coming down," she called out. With foreboding she thought of a kaleidoscope of possibilities -- all disastrous.

On descending she found the troupe around one of the long sofas in the living room. Silva was standing waving his arms explaining in a cascade of Spanish to Pepe who was nodding understandingly at the same time trying to calm him. Pelayo was beside Silva also talking between his pauses for air. On seeing her now at the foot of the stairs followed by Maria, they rushed over to her and the three began talking at once, but Silva's voice dominated.

"Tried to kill me! Now imagine that!"

"'Who?" she asked, remembering Tancat.

"I don't know -- but it was somebody in the house!" He hiked his hastily slipped on pants lacking the belt. A shirt loosely hung outside them, open at the neck revealing a gold chain loaded with heavy dangling medals.

Pelayo, also hastily dressed, though armed with the eternal pince-nez pinned near his shoulder, took over the narrative. "It seems as though the Maestro was in his bed. We had had a late evening after dinner -- all of us were there -- we played cards and chess until midnight. Then they took their leave. The Maestro went up to his bedroom and after being sure all was locked up, I went to mine."

"You live in the villa?" she interrupted.

"Oh, yes," he replied in a tone which told her that his importance naturally included him in Silva's family.

"Then, without warning, there came this cry from the Maestro's room..."

"That's when he tried to hit my head with something..."

"And I immediately jumped up to see -- and this figure -- a man I'm sure -- bumped into me as he ran for the long window, knocked out a pane so much in a hurry was he. And not even thinking about <u>him</u>, I went to see about the Maestro -- if anything had happened to him."

"He only caught me on the shoulder -- the left one, thank God." Paco grumbled, remembering his pain.

But that was my job! She thought as she watched Pelayo solicitously pulling back the Maestro's shirt so all and sundry could see and sympathize. After viewing a dark red mark on the shoulder which would take all of eight hours to heal, she asked Pelayo what she could do to help -- why they had come to her house. Before he could answer, a demanding bell rang from the gate. Pepe sprinted our to answer.

"Watch whom you permit to enter," Paco warned, shouting after him, "God only knows who's roaming around these parts tonight." Then turning to her he asked rather plaintively, "Do you have any cognac?"

"Of course," she went to the nearby bar and looked among the bottles, listening all the while for the approaching footsteps. Pepe entered first and before he could announce him, Gregory Benton followed close on his heels.

"I got the word -- what did happen?" he addressed Paco Silva frowning.

Paco went into his explanation again, aided by Pelayo as before. Benton shot a glance at Miss Bennett who was leaving the bar with a full tray which Maria took to pass around. Then she took a seat on the large couch where Silva and Pelayo had retired.

"I had men posted all around your property," Benton still frowned as he addressed Silva. "I told you many times about your danger. It must have been someone within the house from what you've told me, or one of your groups who did not leave -- who hid and returned to your room later. I was told nobody entered your place, but don't worry. He can't get very far. Too many around to catch him. They told me you both had come here! Why?" He pulled a chair over to sit and face the three of them almost like an exasperated parent. "Why?" he repeated.

"Well, it's just that I trust this lady here..." Silva began in a normal voice, which faded.

"Listen Maestro," stormed Benton pointing at him, "This is exactly what I've predicted all along! You're targeted! I wanted to get you out of here long ago. You could have been killed tonight! Lucky for you it was a bungled job."

"But how was I to know? Why should anyone..."

"For opening your big mouth too wide," Benton interrupted, dispensing with any kid glove treatment. "You've been sounding off about the glories of a now-dead Communism, trying to strengthen the hard-liners. You're due for a trip over there to Russia to give them aid and comfort because of your prestige. Bad-mouthing the new Russian government and all the other governments who shed Communism -- you're a fly in everybody's ointment -- a monkey wrench in the engine. They only love you in Cuba. Maybe you should go there!"

"But..."

"Listen to me. No buts. I've got to get you out of here!"

"You have something to do with the United States government, don't you?" Paco shrewdly asked in his calmest voice so far.

"Right! And a certain other government wants you dead and plans to arrange for us to take the blame. That's it in a nutshell."

There was an uncomfortable pause as all digested this. Maria and Pepe who had listened from the staircase made a small protesting sound. Silva, carefully pursing his mouth lowered his glass to the side table, and to Benton's total surprise looked him directly in the eye and asked, "And how do I know if <u>your</u> government wants me out of the way and will blame it on the top men in power now in Russia? I have often criticized your facade of Democracy too."

"Right on, a fair question," Benton almost smiled, "but we're used to criticism. We don't go around doing away with the critics -- thousands in Latin America and Europe. But I notice they don't mind asking for and getting big bucks from us to save their economy! Don't worry about us. We thrive on criticism."

During this exchange, Miss Bennett although closely listening, still wondered why Silva had come to her villa when there were others closer by. She was soon to have her answer.

"You don't say so!" Silva mockingly commented. "Now you listen! I can enumerate many occasions where your CIA has meddled into governments -- thrown out elected presidents, killed some, paid millions to revolutionaries all to keep Communism -- any branch of it -- blotted out. You can bet they blot it out in Russia, parts of South America, and Asia. Now about tonight..." he paused and put a hand on Miss Bennett's, "the only person I now trust in all of Mexico is this woman next to me -- the lilac and silver lady."

"Mrs. Duran." Pelayo amended.

It was Benton's turn to be shocked. "Her!" he cried.

"Yes, <u>her</u>!" Silva belligerently replied in the same tone.

"Do you know who she is?" unbelievingly Benton looked from Silva to her, and just as surprised, she was looking at Silva. Pelayo was sagely nodding.

"What does it matter who she is," Silva, now in charge, replied. "All I know is she warned me to leave -- she told me I was not safe here. She was without motive – sincere -- I didn't know it at the time, but after what happened, now I feel the truth."

"<u>She</u> told you to leave? <u>She</u> warned you?"

"Yes. Do I have to repeat everything?"

Benton sat back and glared at her. "Is this true?" he asked.

"It is," she replied.

"Do you know this woman carries a gun and is a professional?"

"A professional -- a gun?" Silva chuckled. "And I said I wanted to see her with a gun! But never mind she was trying to protect me. In spite of anything else. I'm staying in this house or wherever she is if she's so professional. Bet she is not with some government! You are! Pelayo, what do you think?" he turned to the secretary.

Adjusting his pince-nez, Pelayo nodded. "I am sure that is the best thing right now, Maestro," he replied. "I have thought about it ever since we came over. Even if it is just temporary."

Miss Bennett stared at the two of them. Benton noticed and commented in English. "You've changed. I don't understand you."

"There's an old song, a spiritual, I believe. It's called, 'You will Understand it Better By and By.'"

"Since he's so determined, could I ask you to put him up here tonight and could I speak to you alone afterwards? It's safe here -- I've had a guard around your house too and whoever was after Silva won't come back anytime soon."

"Yes, I suppose," she replied calling on Maria to prepare two of the bedrooms for her surprise guests.

The telephone began a clamor, all the louder as the room had been quiet for once. Silva had subsided and Pelayo and he were now still sipping cognac. Benton sprang to answer, "I'm expecting a call here," he explained, knowing it to be from Clem whom he had left at Silva's place. All listened as he spoke in English, giving one or two expletives and a grunt before hanging up.

"You won't be bothered from that direction any more," he said to Silva.

"What does that mean?" Silva asked having now recovered some of his authority and was overcompensating for his recent show of fear.

"It means we have your would-be murderer!" Benton replied. He resumed his seat in front of them and began speaking as though to children.

"I don't want to shock you, I'm a bit surprised myself."

"Who? Who would dare?" demanded Silva half rising.

Benton ignored him and spoke to Pelayo. "I want to apologize to you, Sir."

"Apologize to me? I am in <u>your</u> debt. You are helping us -- or trying."

"Who? Who?" Silva insisted.

Benton continued speaking to Pelayo. "It just did cross my mind that it might be you."

"You mean, harm the Maestro -- why, why it's unthinkable!"

"<u>Who</u>?" screamed Silva banging his empty glass on the table.

"Oh, we're getting to that," Benton smiled indulgently. "Mrs. Duran, if you don't mind, I'll have a cognac too."

She silently gestured to Maria who understood.

Benton resumed explanation, still ignoring the fuming Silva. "You see, you were the only other male besides the servants living in the house and, and ..."

"Do not continue," Pelayo muttered shaking his head, very hurt.

"Young man, who tried to kill me?" Silva still demanded.

"It was Professor Henry Parks -- on sabbatical leave who apparently took it into his head to attack you." He finally ended the suspense.

"<u>Henry</u>! But I might have known -- only today he..."

"They found him trying to hide in the potting shed -- the garden house," Benton continued. "He was, of course, outwitted."

Pelayo and the Maestro broke into rapid Spanish which nobody interrupted.

Benton turned and spoke to her in English. "Could I get a few explanations from you?" he asked coldly.

"Of course," she replied.

"I mean after these two gentlemen have been carefully tucked in, since you seem to be their hostess -- at least for now."

At this, Silva who had finished his dialogue with Pelayo rose and repeated his determination to stay, assuring Benton that he had no animosity against him, and nothing reflected on him or his government."

Her heart sank. "But I'm all packed -- I'm leaving on a morning flight, actually in a few hours. It's morning now. But you can stay here in this house, if you wish," she told Silva.

It took a moment for this to be well understood. Then Silva shook his head after a look of confirmation from Pelayo. "Then I will go to New York with you! And Pelayo, too. Right now my instinct tells me what is best to do."

After a shocked silence, Benton smiled at Silva. "Maestro, New York is exactly what I would want for you. You think that's best and so do I, but I would suggest you stay in one of our apartments we keep for these purposes."

"No! No! and No! <u>I</u> will do the arranging. I will stay with this lady, so do not bother about me. I appreciate what you have done, but let me alone from now on, please."

Miss Bennett stared at them in alarm. To be saddled with Paco Silva, famous though he might be, did not appeal to her in the least. What strange quirk had possessed him that she was the only one to be trusted? Only her brief warning to him in the studio? Such a small thing meant so much to him? To cling to her?

As though everything was definitely settled, the two men, guided by Maria who had finished her upstairs work, ascended to their bedrooms.

Bewildered, she turned to Benton as they left. "I'm just as surprised," she said.

"Of all people to trust..." he trailed off reflectively.

"It's impossible," she said ignoring his implication. "It wouldn't do at all."

He regarded her quizzically. "What's this about your warning him? From what I understand, you had other plans for him -- and for me too, I gather."

She sighed, feeling suddenly very tired. "I can't possibly go into anything now.

There's no time. What I want you to know is that I've been sick."

"And I take it you're well now?"

"Exactly. The painting set me straight."

"Things are never as simple as that," he argued. "You have some explaining to do. You can cancel your reservations for today and get some rest, and then we'll talk. And if Paco Silva will get out of town no other way than with you, I would suggest that you be accommodating." There seemed more than a hint of a threat in his tone.

CHAPTER 12

Morning dawned serenely, much to the surprise of everyone inhabiting both villas. It seemed as though the jumbled, hectic events of the night had never occurred. Quiet also reigned in the streets and various patios. Only the telephone lines were busy among Silva's following. The news, of course, spread fast about their colleague, Henry Parks. Morning papers were delivered and the English and Spanish language radio stations began their programs making much of the attempt on the Maestro's life. Also on television, reference was made of an "international plot," or an "anti-Communist zealot" who had confessed, and who would soon be on trial for the ill-advised attempt. A brief shot of Henry Parks trying to avoid the strong camera lights was shown. Now the country would speak in special tones of "The Professor", not needing to name him.

"In other words, I think the Professor did us a favor," Benton mused. Still with no sleep, the two were at Benton's place contentedly listening to the radio's ample broadcast.

"This crazy professor was our biggest unseen advantage..."

"And you should have heard him!" Clem interposed. "He was almost babbling when we took him -- hates Silva!"

"Those people are so unpredictable. Brain-heavy, bad -- very bad."

Pedro came in with their breakfasts, and both were silent as they did justice to coffee, ham and eggs, toast and marmalade.

"I'm going to take a couple of hours sleep, then go talk to her to get to the bottom of this part of the affair."

"Her?" asked Clem even as he knew the answer.

"Yes. Gail Blake who denies being that. Swears she's Heather Duran."

"She's Blake, all right, or I miss my guess," said Clem, "Don't want to rush things, 'specially since there's no direct evidence. Can't pinpoint it yet."

"Right! And it's a damn nuisance too! And this business with Silva wanting to stick to her beats me!" Benton shook his head and pushed away his empty plate.

"Oh well, we knew all the time he's some sort of nut -- when the chips are down, that is."

"Geniuses usually are. He blamed the CIA for foul deeds all over the world, and practically told me I'm not to be trusted, and after all the trouble we've had trying to protect him!"

"Part of the job. So he'll go with her?" Clem asked lighting a self-forbidden cigarette.

"Yes, and it might be right up my alley."

"Why? What gives? He's in no more danger here in Mexico."

"No, not here, but even though there's a contract still out for him up there, I can protect him better in the good old US of A. I know that outfit up there won't back off. They'll try to finish the job, and that's when we can nail the bunch."

"My God! Then he's walking right into the spider's web -- always assuming that she doesn't kill him."

"True, man, true! She's had some kind of a conversion, seems to want out from the job. But it ain't gonna be that easy. Now what with those two together, I think we can draw out the ..."

"The perpetuators?"

"No. We may never get to them -- it's a government -- but at least to the gang -- the syndicate -- the Murder Incorporated -- the family, whichever it is."

"It's bound to be one of the 'families'. Then so what?"

"So at least we did our job and more -- must one little candle..."

"Oh spare me, for God's sake. Look, I'm going to hit the sack for a while. See you around five?"

"Perfect. Is the Professor taken care of?"

"All snug in the local lockup."

"Too bad about him. The real culprit's in another country -- we know that."

"Yeah, but this guy brought it on himself -- practically broke into jail!"

"Bet he'll be a wee bit uncomfortable in a Mexican jail. My guess is at least ten years. Be seein' you -- in all the old familiar places."

The little travel clock pointed to noon. Miss Bennett, alias Duran, awakening, addressed Emily who was napping in her corner bed. "To be alive, alert and able to cope," she said before adding, "I'm in a big hell of a mess, but I get the feeling I can cope."

Emily, thus spoken to, felt free to jump on the bed and have a rare, but appreciated morning chat. She had been fed downstairs, and so felt at peace with the world. Purring she snuggled near the friendly shoulder offered.

"I'm to be stuck -- yes stuck -- with his majesty, his royalty, his serene highness, plus his secretary. Tell me, what have I done to deserve it?"

The cat responded sympathetically.

"They'll interrupt my schedule. My <u>practicing</u>, my music <u>listening</u>. And nobody asked me! <u>Nobody</u>! They all thought I'd be honored. And that pest, Benton just about threatened me to accept that egomaniac in my apartment. I got the message." She paused to scratch Emily's ears. "Tell me, what have I done? All we ask is to be left alone. That's all."

Emily agreed, purred and rolled on her back, hoping she would shortly be brushed for the day.

In spite of complaining to Emily, Miss Bennett anticipated the new day. Gone was the headache, and she successfully held the past at bay. Later she would be capable of fitting the pieces together, and now, it was Gail Blake acknowledging the unforgotten years.

"I really need time for myself," she continued' "More than ever' I plan to sort it out. I have to."

Emily made understanding noises, but as if to remind her, she began to groom herself carefully, stopping occasionally to listen.

"Oh well, let's see what the day will bring'" She rose, showered, dressed, and after brushing Emily's fur, she descended to the breakfast room.

The quiet that reigned told her that neither of her guests was present at the moment. What relief to be alone. She now remembered to cancel her plan reservations and turned her thoughts to the possibility of evading the prospective houseguests in the New York apartment. Although Silva had been adamant last night, she hoped he would now be more flexible with the passing of the night. One of Benton's safe houses would be better for everyone. She was also aware of his ongoing jeopardy, which would continue in New York, but convincing him was another matter.

Then there was this pending meeting with Benton. It disturbed her more than she admitted, for she had no intention of baring her history or her past with him. If she could avoid his probing, she would. Meanwhile, to her surprise, she was hungry, and when Maria appeared, she breakfasted well.

"Good morning, Señora," came Pelayo's voice behind her. She had not heard him on the stain. He smiled as he joined her at the table.

"We are so grateful for your hospitality," he said in his exact, well-pronounced Castillian Spanish. "The Maestro has been terribly treated, and is probably suffering from shock. The brandy last night - this morning, rather, has helped him to sleep late."

"That's good," she replied. "We had a long night."

"And I really think a change would do him good," he continued. "In any case, he believes he is safer with you, and neither I nor anyone in this world will rid him of this idea until he is ready for it."

"I see," she replied with a sinking heart.

"I promise you we will not be a burden. We will, of course, pay our way -- there is no problem there at all. And I take it that your place has extra rooms? He must have plenty of space," he waited inquiringly.

"Well, yes. I have a large apartment -- a floor, in fact, but don't you think the Maestro would be more comfortable in a place of his own? More privacy?" she suggested hopefully.

"But as I told you, he now has the idea that only you can keep him safe- He remembers your warning in the studio, and now that he was told you are a professional with a gun -- that you have security training -- he is determined to stay with you."

"Security training?"

"That is what we understood last night from Mr. Benton," Pelayo said and his pince-nez glistened as in affirmation. She wondered if it had a life of its own.

"Oh, yes," she floundered.

"Then it is arranged. But please, do us the favor of not telling Mr. Benton just where we will be. Does he know your New York address?"

"No, by God!' she jumped up, glad to have found the way out of her mandatory explanation to him. She had been feeling as she had once after an unexcused absence at the music conservatory when she had not practiced sufficiently. Benton was now in the role of her most difficult professor.

"They are clever, those two," Pelayo reminded her. "Are you sure they cannot find us?"

"No. I bought it in another name," she replied, "and I know something about eluding a tail." She started for the stairs and turned quickly. "Can you pack fast?"

"I rose earlier and went to the other villa to pick up some things. We are ready enough. Remember, you said you had reservations for today. The bags are still in the car."

"Good. Get the Maestro ready. We leave just as soon as possible. Keep your luggage in your car. Mine can come down gradually. I would prefer the servants not see. You can help me."

"I understand completely, " he replied, lowering his voice. "The servants think we are leaving tomorrow and we will leave today?"

"Precisely. We can leave from Taxco."

"So they will not be able to tell anything to Mr. Benton and his friend?"

"You guessed it. We're covering our tracks. Your phone is tapped and so is mine. Would you mind that winding road to Taxco?"

"I have driven in Rome, Paris and Madrid," he said proudly. "Mexico presents no problems to me. I drive here all the time."

"We can alternate," she said.

There was a small scene to convince Pepe that he was not needed to drive them. They implied that they wanted to feel quite free to drive down to Taxco leisurely to pick up some silver jewelry. They would be back late evening after lunching there. It would be the Señora's last chance at shopping before leaving tomorrow for New York. Reluctantly he acquiesced thinking how he himself could have enjoyed a Taxco excursion instead of weeding the garden that had been planned that day.

That had been the hardest part; for once leaving Cuernavaca she telephoned from a roadside restaurant to Taxco where she located the charter plane company she had used several years before. They had been prepared to take it from there, but the manager told them to return to a private airport in Cuernavaca where they would be picked up.

At ten that night, they landed triumphantly at LaGuardia. The Mexican pilot would see that the Maestro's car was returned to his villa safely when he himself returned with his plane to Cuernavaca.

Miss Bennett ushered the two men into her twentieth floor penthouse without realizing that beyond airplane trips, Silva had never been in living space at that altitude. He had enjoyed owning and painting in Paris and from various picturesque villas on the Barcelona and French Riviera most of his professional life before settling in Mexico. Now he stepped from the intimate circular foyer into the living room and stopped for a full minute facing the large glass doors leading to the terrace. As in a dream he opened them, stepped out and silently stared.

Watching from inside, Pelayo explained, "We have really never lived so high up. Those lights, and the River! The view is spectacular."

A little surprised, she turned and looked through the doors trying to see it all from their viewpoint. "I like it," she said, "but there are many structures much taller. This building is one of the older ones."

"That may well be, but any taller, the view would not be the same," Paco calculated. "Too high would simply be like being in an airplane."

"I never thought of it like that," she replied. "Now I can appreciate the view even more. Meanwhile, please sit down -- be comfortable. My house is your house," she smiled as she used the familiar Spanish saying before turning to direct the two porters waiting to distribute the luggage.

At that moment, Silva marched into the room, sat beside Pelayo facing the terrace view and finally spoke. "Bring out my sketch book at once. And tomorrow, get me some canvasses -- all sizes!"

Pelayo went to unpack the material, and Silva searched for and found his hostess in another room. Standing at the doorway, he demanded, "Why has nobody told me about this before?"

"About what, Maestro?" she asked, giving him full attention.

"Everybody told me never to come to New York -- too commercial -- the crowds -- people attacking in the metro. Everybody told me that."

"I guess that's part of the city -- part of any big metropolis," she conceded.

"But they never told me about that view out there! And I can't wait to see it in the morning! With the light. The May light!"

"I'm happy you like it -- it's..."

"Like it? My dear lady, it happens to be an inspiration -- a challenge -- maybe a new period in my painting -- it is superb."

"Fine. I'm happy if you are. And perhaps we can come to an agreement. I practice piano daily. I know you paint mornings."

"Oh, I have to paint according to the light. Up here, this spring light -- more northern -- may be entirely different. Also it depends on what I'm working on. You know I am accustomed to my Bach and Beatle tapes. I hope Pelayo packed them." He paused and looked around. "There's a nice piano in here, I notice." He paused making the implication clear.

"Yes, it's my smaller grand, my Steinway. But I use my Bosendorfer concert grand a lot, and that's in the living room."

"We will have to see about that," accepting his offered sketchbook and crayons from Pelayo. "I am accustomed to my tapes," he repeated absently, discarding the subject with ease as he briskly made for the terrace again.

Pelayo and Miss Bennett exchanged telling glances. Pelayo, having understood the significance of the exchange. "I remembered to bring his tapes," he said almost apologetically, but he thinks you can practice on this piano. He doesn't understand the difference. A piano is a piano to him."

"So I notice," she said resignedly. "So I notice."

CHAPTER 13

Within a week of their arrival, Paco Silva, with no trouble at all had converted the terrace and most of the living room into his studio, even unto several half-filled mugs of cold forgotten coffee on various occasional tables. Early on, he had forbidden the intrusion of the customary cleaning services supplied daily by the management. Between his sketching and preparation of a canvas, he had reviewed and approved of the paintings decorating the apartment, two of which were his. But all this had been relegated to minor importance due to the morning view of some tall buildings, touched by sunlight and still clinging to a thin mist which hovered over the East River.

"Pelayo! Mrs.' Duran! God has sent me here!" he announced one day at lunch. They met at lunch and dinnertime for meals ordered from the dining room of the building. "As I told you, this is my New York period. Thank the lord I came -- I should really burn a candle in that cathedral around the corner!"

"Maestro, there is a three hundred sixty degree angle to the terrace," Pelayo said.

"What does that mean?"

"I heard one of the delivery men from the art supply store say that there was a 'wrap-around' terrace out there," Pelayo explained using the English idiom. "It goes around the entire apartment -- beyond those tall plants to the left of your easel."

"Oh, yes, you can have different views," added Miss Bennett. "There's the river view, and on the other side, more of a city view -- buildings."

"Nobody tells me anything!" Silva complained rising at once to check.

"But I am telling him now," Pelayo sighed looking heavenward.

Silva returned in a few minutes declaring, "That terrace gives me many views. It is rich, very rich for me. This apartment is a world apart -- everything is here! The telly in English, French or Spanish, the fine wines from any country, that terrace with an infinity of views!" He sat and resumed his meal.

Miss Bennett nodded in agreement but contemplated the signs of a long visit. Yet, as she went in to practice on the piano assigned to her by Silva, surprisingly, she felt her initial annoyance diminishing.

It was her first chance at the piano since her arrival as there had been readjustments in household arrangements to be made because of her guests, which not only took time, but which diverted her on another path entirely. But now she had established her routine as before, and was happy that Paco Silva had established his with, of course, the help of Pelayo, the invaluable.

She started, as was her custom, with scales in every key, went on to arpeggios, and then began her concerto selected for that day. Two hours quickly passed and as she rose to rest, she was shocked to find Silva and Pelayo standing at the door as though transfixed.

"Mrs. Duran," Silva almost whispered, "What is all this? You are a concert pianist!"

"No, not really -- it's a hobby," she explained. "Do you like other music too besides B and B?"

"Decidedly," he quickly replied. "Mrs. Duran -- forgive me for denying you your favorite piano, and would it be possible -- would it be all right if you did your practicing in the living room so we could hear you? Please?"

She was stunned. The implied compliment overwhelmed her, but she managed to reply normally with a small smile. "I wouldn't want to disturb your work, Maestro, but I will practice there if you wish."

Emphatic assurances were given and, the matter settled, each went back to their respective schedules.

Don Brechenridge, the bartender at the Gold Coin, was worried. The headlines spoke almost daily against some of his favorite customers. It was depressing. He knew what and who they were, but they had been generous to him.

Some were held without bail. The papers wrote about the mafia, the families, murder and such maneuverings that cost the city millions. Don knew that jail for the older men was nothing new, but somehow, they always had gotten out of serving long sentences. But now it seemed as though justice would triumph. Their kingdoms were crumbling. Certain judges had resigned, and sterner judges were on the bench. The outlook was bleak. Don missed the mafia dons, and was careful not to speak of them to the younger men who came in, ate quickly, spoke little and left meager tips.

Anthony and John, the sons of two of the jailed men, were absentminded, preoccupied, and bad-tempered. And no wonder, Don thought. If life imprisonment faced his own father, he'd feel bad too. He tried to give his regular efficient service, riding herd on the two waiters, suggesting and selecting the special wines, all with a view of keeping his normal demeanor, not betraying in any way his cognizance of what had happened.

"Looks bad -- very bad," Anthony said for the third time. They were finishing an excellent meal to which neither had paid much attention. The drinks before and the wine during the dinner helped them to face the truth. The political situation in New York had radically changed. It was now almost impossible to make "arrangements."

"But there must be something we can do," John insisted.

"Chicken soup to Sing Sing," replied Anthony with gallows humor.

"But Papa could always maneuver before!"

"My pop too, but look what's happened to all the capos."

"How did it start? The proof? Did somebody sing?"

"They all sang. All the lieutenants -- I could kill them! First they nabbed that gofer covering the phone deal I set up and went right on from there! Damn! They had been already under heavy suspicion."

"You mean the phone for our little side business?"

"Exactly!"

"And did that ever go through?"

"It did not!"

"And the money -- there's over a million invested there -- what happened?"

"Tancat blew it! It was all in the papers down there and up here too -- don't you keep up with anything? Dumbbell tried to play a lone hand! Botched the whole thing."

"Oh, I read something about that, but never knew that was our basket. But the money -- where's that dead-aim gal with all that money? To buy a couple of pictures. We'd planned to get it back, remember?"

"And that's not all. If we don't deliver that painter, we'll be out of more money failing the contract. They want him dead."

"We could use that bread. Where is he? Can't we still get it done?"

"She's disappeared. It's gonna be harder than ever now with everyone on guard. All hell broke loose down there."

"Maybe she's doubled back to New York after the foul up."

"Maybe. We need the dough now, though."

"Well, check on her -- you still got access to her apartment?"

"Yep."

"Then see about it. Maybe there's a last chance of getting to somebody."

"No way. Our fathers -- God! Do you realize they might be convicted? And at their age, even a few years might mean life for them!"

Without realizing it, Miss Bennett and her guests drifted into a rare sort of domesticity. As the apartment was almost self-contained, the meals delivered silently and on time from the downstairs service, she had time for four or five hours daily at her Bosendorfer with Paco Silva humming along as he worked, and Pelayo, reading, settled in one of the down-pillowed wing chairs with Emily on his lap. Emily, toward the end of the stay in Mexico had been feeling rather neglected with her mistress away so much of the time. But now, she resumed her state of well being. She was in her own home and getting lots of attention. No outdoors, no butterflies to chase around the swimming pool, but still in her own accustomed enclave.

They drifted into a series of strangely ideal days with the Maestro in full command. There were two canvasses he worked on -- one during rainy days, and the other when there was sun.

The three took separate walks on the avenue, though Silva frequently skipped his in favor of the exercise bicycle in the room used as a gymnasium. At night, he devoted himself to the new experience of Spanish language TV in the United States. There were enough stations available to keep him fascinated.

Pelayo had called the Cuernavaca villa on an outside telephone and given instructions. The coterie was not to worry, but to carry on as usual. Checks would arrive to pay all outstanding expenses there. Silva was happy, healthy and productive. He would return when he felt like it, but for now he was wrapped in important projects, and they were to preserve a strict silence. Through some aspect of his personality, Silva in his self-styled new epoch, seemed to have completely forgotten all that had recently happened to him. From the moment he had set foot in the penthouse, he shed the thought of Cuernavaca. He could have been thought to have lived in New York all his life. Also he had made his hostess a fetish of his safety. As long as she was present, he felt untouchable.

Meanwhile, all the self-searching and analysis she had planned had faded. She was now caught up on the piano with her audience of three, including Emily, and was working now on selections she had long ago put aside. It was as though she was preparing for a very important concert. As she had never known how to contact her employers, there was no question of communication. Often as she retired after a day of piano, plus walking and perhaps a concert attended alone at either Carnegie Hall or Lincoln Center, she wondered if that was what was meant by being born again. Far from being bored or irritated with her two guests, she began to wonder how she had lived so contentedly alone for so long.

She noted that her frequent thoughts of Terry, her dead daughter did not evoke the rage and frustration as before. The regret and sorrow seemed more peaceful although still present. She thought of going to the house again, but this time not to pretend to wait for her to come home from school. With time she might be able to close the house. With more time she might be able to sell it. Then she would go to Terry's mausoleum and explain. Terry herself would have wanted that, for she had been practical and even philosophical far beyond her years. If only she had not walked through that wood that day...

On this thought, she tore into a Chopin Polonaise and found she could divert the chain of thought. This had not been possible before that view of "Dama de Lila" as Paco

Silva had named it. She did not realize that Pelayo had looked up from his reading, seeming to sense something different in her mood. It seemed that now, after a month, each was sensitive to the minds of the two others.

She finished the composition and turned to them. "Wouldn't you like to go to the Metropolitan," she asked Silva who had come from the terrace at that moment. "There's a special exhibit you might like to see, and of course your paintings are permanently there too."

"I will get to it, maybe next week," Silva answered, "I was never much for going through galleries when I have a new inspiration. Must complete what I start without undue influences from the past."

"I understand," she answered looking at Silva in his New York persona. Somehow the white duck pants, though paint spattered, and the bright blue open shirt with rolled up sleeves made him more acceptable than the frayed cotton shorts of Cuernavaca.

Pelayo, as usual, wore his summer weight dark conservative suits in the June weather, complete with tie and jacket, and was taken, when he walked out, for a senior New York executive. He was happy because the Maestro was happy. Of course the Maestro could work on anything now and be acclaimed, but it was so different to see him really happy, and of all things, in a new setting -- an entirely new ambiance. Who would have thought it, he daily asked himself. And moreover, the Maestro had always been so prejudiced against New York City. Now look what had happened.

There were some nights when they were together in the living room, half watching television and drinking champagne, making frequent toasts. Pelayo and Silva would begin to reminisce, stopping often to explain the situations to her, enjoying a new audience to impress with escapades, honors, public events, women, film documentaries of which Silva had been the adored subject, and art books of his work.

The news of the mysterious absence of Paco Silva finally leaked, and was carried on television with the cameras focusing on the Cuernavaca group. They photographed very photogenically, but were, as directed, close-mouthed. They implied that the Maestro was working in seclusion and would soon be available to the press.

Also in Cuernavaca Benton and Clem were packing in their respective abodes with the half-defeated feeling of having been made fools of. To this was added the irony of congratulations from Washington for having fulfilled their mission in saving

Silva. It was "mission accomplished" as far as the two of them were concerned. It was felt that no further attempt would be made. When located, vigilance would be kept upon Silva, which would gradually taper off.

"Mission accomplished like hell," Benton grumbled as he threw his clothes indiscriminately into his open bag. "Where the devil could she have got to, and how! I had tails on her too! And they let her get away. Pepe and Maria were wax in her hands! Neither they nor the two tails could stop her."

The phone rang and he answered to Clem's voice. "I'm ready. Car all arranged to be turned in at Mexico City Airport when we arrive."

They caught the New York plane two hours later, and over drinks discussed recent events from the beginning.

"I still don't understand her taking him with her," Clem repeated. "She seemed reluctant to be responsible for him -- imagine his clinging to her!"

"We were to have talked on that morning they left -- can't imagine what happened to her -- said something about having been sick -- something about that picture he did of her too. Wish I could get to the bottom of it."

"I'm afraid you put the watch on the airports hours too late. They had already flown that afternoon."

"Don't rub it in, please. I know that too well. Also know they took a charter -- I checked."

"God knows what else <u>she's</u> capable of."

"'Cause <u>we</u> don't!"

"Well you're on leave now like me. Why continue on that end of the case?

Silva's O.K. Trusts her. She's his gun now. And we got high marks for pegging Tancat -- so called. Don't envy him his time in a Mexican jail. Then you got the credit for spotting the syndicate in New York."

"They'd been under observation a while anyway."

"Yeah, but this hit thing gave FBI the handle."

"I know -- I know, but there's too much left dangling. Got to finish it!"

"You know damn well we're not supposed to work in the States."

"Of course I do."

"Well?"

The pause between them became a silent question.

"O.K. I'm with you," Clem conceded.

"Thanks, old Buddy!"

"But just to keep you out of trouble."

"Don't explain. But thanks!"

CHAPTER 14

That rare day in June came to New York City. The sun lightly enveloped the terrace where Silva was working as usual. The park was showing strong beginnings of unfolding leaves. Further in the distance beyond the tall buildings, the river was visible without the customary shimmer of mist.

Thoroughly appreciating the change the season presented, and anticipating the challenge of yet another vista for his canvas, Paco worked industriously trying to get the most from the morning light.

"Now you will see what a painter I really am," he declared to Pelayo who was sitting at a nearby table with his paper and coffee.

"As though we did not already know what an artist you are," he replied still reading.

Hearing voices, Miss Bennett took a rest from the piano and came out on the terrace. She was wearing yellow silk with dolman sleeves. A string of large amber beads overlapped the high neckline.

Silva hesitated as he observed her, but shook his head. "That color is almost as striking as the lilac on you. But I simply cannot be led astray by your good bones anymore," he concluded as he turned to his work. "I don't know how long this good weather will last."

She turned to resume her practicing, but Silva detained her. "I wanted to ask you before," he spoke a shade diffidently, "tell me why you are not on a concert tour. You are, as one of your poets says, 'wasting your fragrance on the desert air, are you not?'"

She turned, surprised, but quickly recovered. "I didn't want it badly enough -- the sacrifice, the dedication, the traveling -- giving up everything to art. In any case I had all that when I was a kid -- a prodigy. It was horrible! The pressure."

"And so you got married, I suppose," Silva's tone was condescending.

"Exactly," she replied ignoring the deprecation. "I knew precisely what I wanted, and when my parents died, I decided to do what I wanted."

"Then why take the trouble to finish at a top conservatory?"

"I played by ear. But I was desperate to learn the right way -- by note."

"By ear?"

She was spared the explanation by Pelayo who patiently designated the difference of memorizing a heard piece of music and being able to read the piece from written notes on the musical staff.

"Ah," breathed Silva, "I never dreamed of the difference. And so many of my friends play. I wonder if they can read the music."

"I think they all can, Maestro," Pelayo replied, "since they are world famous." He named a few, exchanging smiles with Miss Bennett.

"You never regretted marriage and dropping the career?" Silva persisted, ignoring Pelayo.

"Never," she replied. "We had a few good years together. I wouldn't trade them for anything -- much less a career -- anyway, I'd already had one."

Both men regarded her with renewed interest. To the women they knew who had the genius to support a career, marriage came second. They waited expectantly not wanting to ask what became of the marriage.

"He was killed in the Iran Marine debacle," she added anticipating their thought, and marveling that she could now talk to them about it. "And later," here she hesitated, "my young daughter was killed too."

Sounds of sympathy from them both came as she left them, went to the piano and began a soothing Schubert melody, realizing she felt better after talking. The song soothed, almost healed, and was just demanding enough to awaken interest for her fingers and memory.

Silva sighed and shook his head as he continued on his painting. "So much work to be done -- so much to finish," he murmured. But his thoughts were with Miss Bennett. How could he have thought she was silver and ice? This woman had a heart.

Pelayo was even more touched. He scooped up Emily to her delight and sat in his now favorite wing chair to listen. The cat purred and settled down for her midmorning nap surrounded by all the attention she felt she deserved.

An hour later, the ring of the intercom from the main floor came as an unwelcome interruption. She had a presentiment which was realized when she answered the house phone.

"A gentleman on his way up, Ma'am," the doorman spoke apologetically. "I couldn't stop him -- said he was your friend and you wouldn't mind. I think I've seen him before."

In the interval between the expected ring of the door, she thought desperately of Paco Silva, so innocently painting, so secure, so sure of his safety, for her instinct told her it was her employer as there was never a bona fide visitor at the penthouse.

The buzzer rang and on opening she saw a tall, darkly good-looking man. He was young, and though dressed and groomed impeccably, there was something about his one- sided smile that she did not like. They gazed critically at each other for an instant.

"I don't think I know you," she said.

He moved inside as though familiar with the place and she led him toward the small room used as a gymnasium.

"You know me," he countered. "Remember the little notes in the magazines? I'm the one who gives you your assignments."

They stood for a moment as he looked around expectantly.

"Well, please sit down," she pointed to a chair. "I'm glad you came. I've been waiting."

"Bad luck in Mexico," he commented lighting a cigarette.

"Yes, Tancat jumped the gun -- my gun, that is."

"Did you bring back the money?"

"Yes. I have the picture money and I'm returning your expense money. Of course I don't expect to be paid."

"There's no need to return the expense money," he said rather grandly although instantly regretting it.

"I insist. Thanks just the same, but I'm retiring from the profession."

"Retiring!"

"Yes, Mr....?"

"Never mind the name," his smile disappeared. "I don't understand."

"It's very simple," she spoke as though to a retarded person. "I've finished with the profession. Also I'm concentrating now on my music."

"But that spoils your whole career!" he exclaimed, "I was going to give you more assignments -- even now if you can locate this artist, you can still have the job!"

A cold fear swept over her. She felt like a mother whose child has been threatened. She had to protect Silva. Nobody was going to harm him. He depended upon her for safety and she was going to see that he remained safe. This hoodlum must go. She wondered if it would be better to rid the world of his ilk.

"As I say," he continued, "you can play music in your spare time. Why waste your talent!"

She smiled at his priorities. Her talent indeed.

Her earnestly pursued his point. "You're turning down more than a million, considering your future!"

"I already have a million," she replied.

He considered the logic of this a moment and could think of no quick answer. She gestured him to wait and hurried to her bedroom where from a small wall safe, she extracted two envelopes. Returning, she handed them to him. Meanwhile, he had risen and was pacing the room as he smoked.

"I'm disappointed in you," he finally told her after carefully counting the money.

"Sorry," she answered, her manner belying her words. She had earlier realized that he was a person needing to maintain the ascendancy in any situation. Any slight vibration could trigger some unpleasantness and she wanted to be rid of him as soon as possible. God forbid that Silva or Pelayo should show themselves before he left. It was clear he did not know their whereabouts.

At last he reluctantly headed for the door. 'Let me know if you change your mind." There was an edge to his voice. "In any case I'll be contacting you from time to time just to see."

"If you don't mind wasting your time," she answered leading him out. "Thanks for everything."

"That's O.K. But you think it over." He was at the door, turned and smiled knowingly, then left.

She stood a moment to collect herself and gave a shudder of disgust. Poor Heather Bennett, she thought. Bitter, deadly automaton, thank God she was dead or dying. She hoped there would be no necessity to recall her to life.

Anthony was thoughtful as he left the building. It was a disappointment to lose a good gun like her. So safe, so dependable, so anonymous. Her jobs were well done with no complications. Imagine her preferring music. Some people had no respect for business. He might have known a woman would be frivolous. And the money! Yet another something kept tugging at his memory of the visit -- something rather odd. What was it? He passed a large luxury toy store and stopped a moment to look in the display window. Among the atomic, blasting, killing-type mechanical specimens well presented, beautifully arranged, he noticed a harmless child's painting set nestled between a monster from outer space and an explosive contraption supposedly about to blot out the world in twenty seconds. Now it came to him. It was the small of paint noticeable in the foyer of her apartment. A heavy oily paint -- not the kind used in home decorating. Could it be she had reneged on this job and had made friends with that painter fellow – what about those paintings in her living room -- was she partial to art? Oh, Hell! What a good gun gone bad. He would look into it -- worth a try. He had read somewhere he was in hiding. Perhaps he'd discovered the unlikely hiding place.

He was distracted by the flash of a camera in his face. It had not been the first time this had happened. Two long human-interest stories had appeared in one of the more spectacular evening tabloids about the families of the two men indicted. He minded, but not too much. Give him two or three years, and he would show them. He'd show them all.

CHAPTER 15

The house in Englewood contained the synthesis of the personalities of Gail and Theresa Blake. Both Benton and Clem knew it the first fifteen minutes. They had entered at midnight, surreptitiously. The quiet, almost isolated neighborhood seemed completely deserted -- sleeping, waiting calmly for daybreak when its life would again take on meaning, would begin its slow not unpleasant march toward completion.

They found the place small -- almost a cottage. The furniture seemed to have been bought second-hand and expertly refinished. The upright piano with its music etudes for secondary students gleamed in the lamplight. The carpet was old, but Persian. Moving along to the other rooms of the one-story structure they found two bedrooms, furnished as they had noted on covers of women's magazines.

They saw several framed photographs, in the typical bedroom of a young couple -- the man in uniform, the woman a slightly younger and happier version of Gail Blake. The uniform carried the insignia of a Marine captain. The modest room was as though waiting for them to return. The bed cover was a hand-crocheted spread with tassels reaching to the floor. The dressing table carried powder, perfumes, cosmetics and a tortoise shell set of comb, brush and mirror. All seemed spotless, as though someone had only recently left and was expected back any moment.

Benton opened the top drawer of the chest-on-chest and recoiled at its contents. Inside was an open box of medals and several ribboned decorations, but his eyes lingered on the purple heart. Beside these was a bulky object which he recognized as the American flag, folded precisely as the guard of honor folds it when it is taken from a hero's casket and presented to his widow before the casket is slowly lowered. He gently closed the drawer and looked into the closet where he saw mixed clothing and another uniform. An eerie feeling crept along the back of his neck. He glanced at Clem inspecting the other drawers and could sense his mood. Both were thinking how much they felt intruders.

"This house doesn't seem to be the home of a woman like her," Clem almost whispered. "It's too middle-class -- too homey."

"What I'm now sure of," Benton replied, pausing, "is this is Gail Blake's home. She's changed into somebody else. She must keep this for the memory -- but it's uncanny. They say she doesn't live here -- just comes occasionally."

"Why would she be wanting to do that, I wonder," Clem muttered.

They entered the second bedroom. Here there were frilled curtains, a tennis racket on the wall, group pictures of teenagers on the draped heart-shaped dressing table. A ruffled counterpane of organdy matched the curtains, and the upstanding pillows, also ruffled. A radio and a flounced lamp stood on the night table. And on the wall was an enlarged snapshot of a face -- a laughing face with windblown hair, completely unselfconscious that a camera was near.

"There's quite a resemblance," Clem said. "We know for sure now with the pictures she's the same woman. But why would she keep it all intact like this. It isn't normal!"

"That's the whole point," Benton replied, "it isn't normal -- that's why she's 'bent'."

"Bent?"

"The neighbors say not only did she lose her husband in that Iran Marine tragedy, but the daughter was raped and murdered later."

"Yeah, I remember -- guess that's enough to send anybody off the track."

After examining more closets, books, music albums and drawers, their feeling of guilt increased.

"Let's get out of here," Clem suggested. "We can put a watch on the place in case she comes any time soon."

Benton nodded and turning off all the lights, after trying to leave things as they found them, they softly closed the front door whose lock they had expertly picked, walked to their car, parked further down the street and headed for the George Washington Bridge.

She could tell he had kept something back. She faced the daytime doorman who, at her bidding had come up to her apartment. They were sitting in the same room in which she and Anthony had talked. Tall and distinguished in his sky-blue uniform, Fred held his cap nervously in his lap as he answered her questions. Yes, her recent visitor had returned and had asked about her. What had he told him? Nothing much, just that she did have company from foreign parts -- that was all. He seemed to have known it in any case. The gentleman had been so insistent that he, Fred, had gotten suspicious and had sent him on his way.

"I see," she said looking directly at him.

He wished she would not do that because her eyes seemed to look through him. He hoped she did not guess about the hundred-dollar bill exchanged.

"If I've been indiscreet," Fred smiled weakly, now aware of the more than generous tips she had given him over several years, "please excuse me. I didn't mean to blab -- it was just that..."

"And what else did he ask you?" she interrupted.

"Nothing important -- just a few details about your guests which I, of course, did not answer."

"I see. Well, thank you, Fred." She rose to dismiss him.

He was disconcerted, knowing now that his future tips from her were at great risk, and that wouldn't do at all. His vacation was coming up right in line with his birthday of which he never failed to remind his old established tenants, and this lady who always kept to herself had never failed him. And then there was Christmas! Oh, God!

"If I've done wrong, please excuse it," he repeated getting to his feet. "I had no idea there was any harm..."

She led the way to the foyer. "It's just that I thought your professionalism would be on the line in such a case," she told him. "Throughout the years I've known you I was sure you protected my privacy. A bit of a let down."

She could not have said anything to wound him more. He well knew the written and unwritten laws of his job, and the greater of these was often the latter. He backed out the door still apologizing and inwardly cursing his weakness in taking the man's money when he had now jeopardized three or four times that much with his big mouth.

On his departure, she sat for a few minutes in deep thought. Then she returned to the piano near which, as usual, Pelayo was sitting reading and holding a half-sleeping Emily. Silva stood at his easel just outside on the terrace.

"How about something by Albeniz?" she asked. "Something Spanish."

"I always liked his work -- Cordoba, for instance -- but Mrs. Duran, I supposed you know -- I am Catalan, born in Barcelona. We once had our own country, you know-Now we're all supposedly Spanish."

"You have your own language and literature too -- yes, I know. I also realized from your name -- an ancient Catalan king, right?"

"Right," he repeated, surprised at her knowing.

"And speaking of names," she went on, leafing through her music for her Albeniz folio," I wish you and the Maestro would call me Gail. Not Mrs. Duran any more – just Gail. Please."

He nodded, again surprised, but politely accepted this new state of affairs. Somehow he could not bring himself to ask her to drop the title of Señor from his name. It was sudden, this change, and after all although very talented, still she was a woman and younger than he, and in any case, he would add the Señora. She would be Señora Gail. It would not do to be otherwise, and he would still be Señor Pelayo.

She began the piece she had located and as she went into the thoughtful, almost dreaming introduction, she thought how helpful the song was. It suited her well; the mood evoked was peaceful, soothing, enabling her to know that she must now take on her last job. It was the only sure protection for the Maestro and it would be done by Gail Blake. By sheer luck she had seen Anthony's picture in the *Times* the day before, and the compete and exhaustive article left little to guess. His father was coming to trial within two days, and she decided to be sure to be among those present at court.

Anthony paused while dressing. The dark red tie might go well with the charcoal gray custom-made suit, but on the other hand -- he gave a quick snort -- so many decisions, even this. It had always been like this, even in the one college to which he had been able to achieve admission. His was always the deliberate choice, the effort to do or select the right thing. He envied the others who seemed to be able to breeze through the world without apparent effort or thought, always hitting the right note, quick with a clever quip, the riposte, without thinking twice. Also they gave the right answers in class without too much study, but everything he had ever done in that rather alien place had been the result of digging, hard thought, deliberate effort. It had cost him a lot, for though he did manage to get through, he had never really achieved entrance into the elite of his class neither academically nor socially. It was something his father had never guessed, as proud as he was of him. A college graduate in the family -- and his son and heir!

Now look how the empire had crumbled. They had attached practically everything. It was a shame -- his father had worked so hard for success. Never mind the means he had taken to achieve what he wanted. The end justified the means in this case. His father could do no wrong -- he had even paid many thousands in taxes. It was a plot against the family and his father as a self-made leader had to take the rap for them all.

And now, of all things, money -- real money had become scarce and hampered further efforts at bribery or elimination of witnesses to wring out the very last chance either to get an acquittal or to plea bargain for a lighter sentence. Money was mandatory, and it might come to his having to do several pending jobs. Perhaps it was better if he would do the Silva job himself saving the fee. Once or twice his father had let him go stalking with one of the experienced guns just to get the hang of it -- starting at the bottom so to speak, and he was sure he could manage it.

He ran downstairs to greet his mother who was waiting breakfast for him. Even though there had long been enough money to hire household help, she wouldn't hear of it -- nor did she permit them to leave their comfortable but modest home in a middle class section of Long Island for anything like they could have afforded.

"This is my real home," she often intoned, "and nobody's going to make me change it for chromium and plastic and crazy architecture!"

They let her have her way and had become accustomed to it. Only a professionally laid out vegetable and flower garden bespoke their nod to over-spending, for she had threatened to plant one herself, and her requisite had been an arch of a grape arbor where they sat on summer evenings over dinner and wine.

She was now tearful, and had vacillated between going to court or staying at home all morning. Anthony hoped she would keep at home -- thus minimizing any display of grief she would be sure to exhibit on seeing her husband. Anthony was extra solicitous this morning, eating a full breakfast to her approval, and catching her around the waist as she waited on him with frequent sighs.

"No need to worry, Mom," he kept telling her, "He'll be out in no time at all." His false cheer rang hollow, but he insisted. "I'm seeing a couple of key people today." He accepted another helping of omelette. "Please take hold of yourself, Mom -- no need to cry!"

He prepared to leave, but his heart sank as he saw her remove her apron and go for her coat and hat.

"I think I should go," she explained as she hurriedly shrugged into the coat and put on her hat without a mirror.

At last they were out of the house on their way to the courthouse of the trial and as he drove, he mentally counted his liquid assets and the amount of money and time needed to reach his key people. Adding, multiplying and dividing, he came up with the fact that he must eliminate Silva himself, and he now knew Bennett was shielding him. It must be soon. He was sure he could do it alone. The government who was paying him did not really care who or what accomplished the hit. Just so the hit was made. Silva must be shut up.

With the advantage of having been able to enter the apartment in the past to pay her when she was away from the premises, and in the light of his large tip to the doorman there, he began to hope.

Should it be the new Cardin model which she had ordered and had found waiting for her on her return from Mexico, or should she take the role of a camera person on assignment and dress more simply? The cameras would offer more opportunities for her job, she decided, so she selected a green moleskin skirt with a short dark green leather jacket and a white silk blouse. Flat-heeled tall boots completed the outfit. She already possessed cameras.

Then she carefully took her twenty-two from its chamois bag and checked it. It was lovely with its beautiful sheen, still loaded and still striking with the gleaming sapphires. She sighed, noting the difference in her feeling for the bauble. Both the gunsmith and the jeweler had excelled themselves, and it was probably worth more than ever to a collector. But now, at this moment to Gail Blake, it was just another piece of excellent work, not a substitute for a life. And now, Gail Blake must finish Heather Bennett's important job.

The scene outside the courtroom verged on the frantic. A man twice acquitted was now again on trial with one of his former lieutenants turning State's evidence. "Gentleman Joe", as some of the tabloid press often called him, had begun to take on legendary good luck. The fact that he photographed well contributed to his image. The papers showed a tall, well groomed, even distinguished figure with his well-cut gray hair almost a trademark, his benign expression belying the murder accusations of the hostile witnesses.

Everyone wanted a seat in the courtroom as there was a feeling, an undeniable something in the air that this time would be different. Had Gentleman Joe's luck run out? Here might be history in the making. Those seeking entrance included grandmothers, secretaries on French leave, retirees, salesmen who could reroute territory, law students, and of course, family and friends of the defendant which were considerable, as outside, there was even a demonstration of these carrying placards extolling the character and past life of the man who was now pictured as a martyr.

Later all converged into the building hoping for room. If history was to be made they wanted to witness it.

Into this came Anthony and his mother, he hurrying her along as they mounted the steps before she could make a scene either of grief or of anger at some of the audible comments around her, for on one side he was heard to be an average family man, never ostentatious, generously giving to worthy charities and active in his neighborhood causes. In a marked difference of opinion, others were calling attention to the various monopolies he headed, the frequent demises of certain of his associates, and his clinging to the myth that he was a law-abiding owner of a modest bakery and paid taxes on said business -- ha!

A woman photographer aimed her camera at him, as did many others including the television cameras. Miss Bennett thought it would not hurt to gather some credibility around herself, to see and be seen among the fourth estate for a while. In any case never would she make the hit while the woman, so obviously his mother, was with him. There would be time enough to do it, as she win sure the woman would not accompany him every day of the trial. She snapped diligently, working two cameras professionally, taking various positions, as did the others, also following the other photographers when they spotted someone they thought important to the trial. It was almost too easy, she thought, and then, as she turned triumphantly from a full-face shot of Gentleman Joe himself stepping from the car with his guards, she froze. Benton, the last person she thought of or wished to see, was also gazing at the prisoner, commenting to Clem beside him.

Against her will she felt her heart accelerate, but insisted to herself it was simply blood pressure. The thick chestnut hair now shining in the summer sun, the penetrating brown eyes seeming to miss nothing, the determined chin, all too familiar and she would later hate herself for feeling uncomfortable. What was her problem? Whatever he suspected, he could prove nothing against her in spite of that phone tap. At this moment, he must not hinder her plan and in spite of his presence, she must take advantage of the days of the trial to act. He had not seen her, for he and Clem, as everyone, were focused on the man of the day as he made his way between his husky escorts into the building. She casually turned and walked away, shifting the cameras to her shoulders after placing them carefully in their cases. She would go home and try again the next day, but this time warily. If he saw her now, her plans would be in ruins.

"Seems a harmless sort of guy -- kind to his mother -- ideal family man, eh?" Clem commented as he and Benton left the courthouse later.

"That's why he's suspect in my book," Benton laughed. "Got to watch those 'kind to the family' types, right?"

"Damn right," Clem replied. "Let's have a drink. I know a good bar near here where they make 'em strong! And after all, we're supposed to be on vacation. Here we are still working. And on our own, too!"

"O.K. But I had a feeling she'd be in court today -- after all, those people were her bosses."

"Yeah, but did she know that?" Clem asked.

"Thought she'd guess -- since her hotline in Mexico was cut off pretty sudden and then the publicity of the indictment -- dovetailed."

They discussed the various possibilities as Clem led with the instinct of a homing pigeon to his bar, the outside of which was unprepossessing, but the interior intimate, spotted with its special customers who enjoyed its casual feeling, its lack of garish decorations, its comfortable seats and tables, its muted music, and its privacy.

"You've spoken with Cuernavaca?" Silva asked as Pelayo entered smiling.

"Yes, Maestro -- I did and they want your permission to show "La Dama de Lila.""

"Oh yes, I'd almost forgotten. I'm so busy here. It was finished. I would only have ruined it if I had done more on it. Pierre can put my protector on. My invention."

"Yes, I know."

"And what else?"

"A week at Bellas Artes arranged in Mexico City before it comes north to the Met."

"The Met!"

"Oh, the Metropolitan Museum of Art, Maestro -- it's just that I'm getting accustomed to talking the New York way."

"They say the 'Met'?"

"Yes, and that could mean the opera House too -- that's the Met too."

"I see. It's good to know all these things. But Pelayo, let's get back to the Met -- the art gallery -- what's this about my picture coming there? That's why your walks are longer every day. You've arranged something there without my permission or knowledge!"

"Maestro," Pelayo threw up his hands, "They are giving it a special place near the entrance -- special lights and everything. I thought it would be best if I explained it all to you when it was arranged -- just to see if you would approve or not. I thought if you could imagine it all in the perfect setting instead of being bothered with details..." He tapered off, anticipating the usual reaction.

Inwardly very pleased, Silva continued a moment on his painting -- the park with its leaves, now fully open, the buildings and the river beyond, which he was beginning to love. Suddenly he shrugged and raised his eyes heavenward to imply that it was none of his doing. If they wanted to show his work, who was he to demur? He was the modest one. If the disciples -- his secretary and all the rest -- insisted on placing him before the public, what could he do?

Five minutes passed during which Silva continued working and Pelayo waited.

"And what else?" Silva finally asked.

Pelayo gave his special smile. "I was just thinking, Maestro, only an idea, mind you, what an interesting thing it would be - really unusual..."

"Get to the point, Pelayo!"

"Yes, of course. Well if you would appear briefly at the private opening! What a coup! You at the debut of your latest work of art, and if..."

"If what?"

"If we could only get the Lilac Lady to come..." he stopped as he saw Silva stop work and rest his brushes.

"You seem to have arranged it all."

But Pelayo knew when he had planted the fertile seed and well knew what would be decided.

An animated conversation followed during which by some subtle magic which had earned him an invaluable post for many years with Paco Silva, Pelayo's idea gradually turned into the Maestro's idea, and now it remained for the many details to be finished, not the least of which was broaching the subject to Señora Gail, as they both now called her.

CHAPTER 16

"We just haven't upped the ante enough!" Anthony declared as he and John met at the Gold Coin after the first day of court. He had seen his mother home, and had headed immediately back to the restaurant to discuss strategy with John, whose own father would be on trial shortly.

"But my contacts have been completely messed up. They were even threatened with jail for offering bribes. It's impossible, I tell you!"

"You give up too soon," Anthony scoffed, accepting their chilled cocktails.

"If we offered enough money -- say a million -- I bet we could swing it. If the damn bleeping lieutenants hadn't backed out!"

"Everyone's running for cover after Tony turned State's evidence -- you know that!"

"Whatever happened to the oath -- to loyalty?"

"God only knows."

"Well I'll see what I can do on my side to raise more," John finally conceded. "But what about you? We've got a hell of a lot tied up in the Mexico deal!"

"I got it back from her," Anthony said, "she's chickened out anyway. A good gun gone sour!"

"Chickened out!"

"Yeah, chickened out -- said she was concentrating on her music."

John set his glass down hurriedly. "You mean you went there? She saw you?"

"Yeah, I went there -- wanted to see what happened -- everything came up such a big mess."

"But good God! Don't you see what you've done? You've left yourself vulnerable. When she'd never seen your face -- it was a thousand times better. Now she might be traced -- made to talk and testify against all of us. Plus that your picture's been plastered all over the papers -- she could recognize you! Who you are! Pinhead!"

"Oh plenty can testify against us, and are. Why pick on her?"

The dinner came at this point. They devoted themselves to it for a few minutes.

"It's not just one thing -- it's everything! She's not our type -- not born into the business -- from everything you tell me. You said she had those expensive pictures -- those pianos..."

"What's that got to do with it? She was a good gun -- my best one."

"Yeah, but there had to be a catch in it with somebody like that- She's no run-of-the-mill gun. She could be dangerous!"

"Well just what would you suggest I do? I plan to do the Silva job myself in any case. That gives us a good start! We keep what we would have paid her."

"And while you're at it, do the job on her too. Better for us all around."

Anthony thought about this a moment. "What's one more? I can do a double if it protects us."

"Let me know if you need any help. Can you be the lone ranger?"

"Trust me."

She knew something important was pending the moment she entered. Pelayo looked up expectantly as he greeted her from his winged chair, half rising and unceremoniously sliding Emily from his lap. Paco Silva craned his neck toward the room from his stance on the terrace and made preparations to cease working. Even Emily purred expectantly around her ankles, sniffing curiously at her boots.

"You're back!" Pelayo exclaimed. "We were waiting to tell you the news!"

She rested her cameras, dropped her jacket and sank in a chair to remove her boots. Emily, dispersing her favors equally, now jumped in her lap.

"What's new?" she asked.

"A big surprise, Señora Gail," I wanted you to know when I had made all the arrangements. I have been in contact with the Met."

"The opera people?"

"Oh, no, the Metropolitan Museum. I did not say anything to you or the

Maestro about it until it was all set as a definite thing."

Something in his manner warned her they would ask a favor. Silva came in from the terrace and made a production of selecting a cigarette, seating himself and lighting up. He listened to Pelayo as though hearing it for the first time.

"And within three weeks," Pelayo finished, "it can be here in New York. Special opening, special lighting, special attention -- press conference and everything. When I do something, I do it thoroughly, of course."

"That's just wonderful!" she told them. "I congratulate you. I can't imagine a better debut." While he was speaking she had mentally reviewed the projected dates of her last project and had calculated that her erstwhile employer would no longer then be a threat. Surely she could complete her work before then.

"And we thought of another good idea..."

"Oh, no, Pelayo," interrupted Silva, "you thought – it's all your idea, I knew nothing about it until about fifteen minutes or so ago!"

"Of course, Maestro. But Señora Gail, I thought it would be such a marvelous idea if you were to appear in the same lilac dress and sit for two or three minutes beside the picture!" His pince-nez actually seemed to gleam hopefully at her.

She had feared this. "And what about all this privacy we needed -- all that running from Gregory Benton and his pal. You know he's with the government, I think the CIA. What about all that?"

"That organization cannot function within the US limits," Silva surprisingly announced. And anyway I can make my big announcement rejecting Communism at the affair. Both you and

Benton said that was what was needed. To stop criticizing the new Russia and renounce!"

She looked at him unbelievingly. Pelayo exclaimed in Catalan, then went over to give Silva a congratulatory abrazo.

"Enough, enough, Pelayo -- so dramatic -- what does it matter who's Communist or not. I admit I was stubborn. After all art is more important than politics. Art will last forever. Politics will change with the wind!"

"That's what everyone was trying to tell you," she smiled, greatly relieved, and thinking that the one blow Tancat gave him in Cuernavaca worked miracles. It must have been then when he realized his danger, and weighed the consequences of his intransigence.

"And if I am to make such a sacrifice -- such a change, Señora Gail, could you make my exhibit unique by sitting beside the picture in the lilac dress -- a few moments only?"

Again they both looked hopefully at her. She lifted Emily to her shoulder to gain a little time, but even then she knew her answer. "All right," she agreed, "provided there's absolutely no publicity about the private showing, I'll do it. But absolutely no publicity, mind you. And never, never mention my name to anyone!"

They were effusive, the Maestro approaching to kiss her on both cheeks. "We do not really know what your name is, Señora," he laughed. "First, Mrs. Doran, now Señora Gail, and sometimes I see periodicals on the tables addressed to a Miss Bennett, and also that's on the index in the lobby."

"In New York, you can call me Señora Gail Blake," she replied slightly disoriented by the Maestro's kiss. "I am really Mrs. Gail

Blake, but my security work makes me have to change my name from time to time'"

Silva turned, went for a bottle of champagne which he happily proceeded to open and serve. "One thing, however," she mused after her first sip, "We must invite Mr. Gerard -- the man who made the lilac dress. He would be so happy."

CHAPTER 17

Anthony began to realize that his decision to accomplish the double liquidation was good in theory, but quite another thing to get the time to make the necessary preparations. The trial was on in full force, and his mother had decided to attend every day. His sources still had no luck in reaching the right people in spite of increased incentive, for both Anthony and John were still seeking new avenues to help the situation. His father appeared in court daily, well groomed, but obviously depressed and looking much thinner and years older. Each day seemed to take a heavy toll as conviction seemed inevitable.

Gail Blake's frustration was also present as, in spite of the excellent opportunity as a news photographer, aiming the camera at her target, she always encountered his mother at his side, and there was no question that she could not do it under those circumstances. Once she even trailed the two to a restaurant during a break in the proceedings, but the mother kept close at all times to her son. She well knew Anthony's plans for both herself and Silva, and faced the necessity of being the first to act.

Meanwhile she had tried to curtail the Maestro's excursions from the apartment, infrequent though they had been, painting a not too exaggerated picture of the danger of the streets of New York. She had also been severe with the three doormen who alternated their shifts.

Then unexpectedly, the trial was over, crowned with a conviction. The overwhelming evidence was there and the mandatory sentence of twenty-five years was passed. Caught by surprise, wondering about her next move, she knew she must accelerate her plans.

Meanwhile, engrossed in her all-important dilemma, the date of the debut of the painting took her by surprise. Although the news had spread throughout the art world and beyond, she had been too preoccupied to concentrate on it. Now, two days before the event over which Pelayo and the staff and the museum had worked so hard to achieve, she was faced with the reality of what she was expected to do.

The preliminary visit for a look at the results of the efforts of the lighting engineers, the decorators, and the arrival of the painting was impressive. The three approved of the platform covered in velvet, the exact duplicate of the chair in the painting, the angle of the painting in relationship to the platform, and the angle of the platform in relation to the entrance. Located in a recessed area of the spacious lobby, the tableau still dominated, instantly visible from the entrance and now awaited only the final touches of the decorators and the last minute flower arrangements.

She refused to look again at the painting, remembering her reaction the one time she saw it, and more and more she dreaded her chore, five minutes though it might be, of duplicating the pose for the invited public. She listened as Pelayo and Silva congratulated the staff on the selection of the frame, the colors of the lighting, and on the perfection of the entire concept. They were both happy, but hers was the responsibility for keeping him alive. Clouding the proceedings was her worry that the Maestro's planned renunciation of his long- held and widely extolled political philosophy would not be in time to rescind the contract put out for him months ago. Somehow the danger she herself faced was taking secondary importance.

Although the early summer weather had so far been normal for New York, the day of the private showing dawned as that poetic, fabled rare day in June. The temperature slid from a cool moderate to an even more pleasant moderate and held. Manhattan continued ideal as day faded into evening.

Into an exquisitely decorated apartment in the east mid-fifties, evening was bringing what was approaching a crisis. As creator of the lilac dress, although usually her coiffeur, Mr. Gerard had been delighted to receive his client, Miss Bennett's, invitation with a covering note explaining her role as model of the now famous picture, and the fact she had worn his creation in it.

Now, evening was falling, the evening of the debut of the picture, no less, and neither he nor his friend who shared his apartment had made their decisions as to what they would wear. A burnt umber crushed velvet pair of trousers with matching jacket lay on the bed next to a violet moiré suit. Both looked and deliberated.

"A disaster," pronounced Mr. Gerard. "If we're to attend together, our outfits would clash and clash terribly. It would never do!"

"Then what about dinner clothes?" his friend suggested-

"Oh, I'm sick of those dark colors -- like a bunch of penguins!"

"Yes, but..."

"And had I known in time, I could have made myself a lilac outfit to match the dress I made for her."

His friend, Arlyn considered a moment. "No that would be tacky -- so obvious -- you in lilac too!"

Gerard turned to check his hairstyle in the nearby mirror although it had been perfect throughout the day. It crossed his mind that Arlyn had recently been rather critical -- or on the edge of being critical. He himself was more than usually nervous and thus more sensitive, but just the same, he suspected a streak of jealousy in Arlyn's recent manner-

"Well, we do want to be noticed," Gerard concluded. "But I suppose it would be better to go for the dinner jacket. At least I can wear my wine one with the cummerbund contrasting."

"I'll wear my gray one then."

"I've been thinking, Arlyn. This may be my cue to think about going into haute couture!"

"Why not? But it takes a fortune to get started."

"Yes, but imagine the publicity I'll get tonight! My dress painted by Paco Silva!"

The gala began. The magic blend of the rich, the beautiful, the distinguished, the important, and the talented gathered in the incredibly arranged reception area of the Metropolitan Museum. Everything merged into the perfection of an ambiance rarely achieved even at that level.

Silva's and Pelayo's entrance was well-timed and their impact in the distinguished receiving line was great as they were placed among leading financiers, politicians, artists, and socialites.

Into this extraordinary scene came two pairs of uninvited guests who had with a little difficulty succeeded in maneuvering entrance. Benton and Clem Johnson were impressed in spite of themselves, and assumed the role of men-about-town, circulating while awaiting their change to approach Paco Silva. Anthony and John, exhibiting a combination of charm and lies about a forgotten invitation, let another hundred-dollar bill add a certain verisimilitude to the situation. They too circulated, and though impeccably dinner jacketed, immediately knew they were out of their depth. Any lingering thought Anthony might have had concerning completing the Silva contract was canceled. The look that passed between them on entering settled that. Yet they lingered, tasting the heady atmosphere though they realized they could never really be a part of it.

Behind the scenes in an improvised dressing room, Gail Blake was wondering why she had ever let herself be talked into such a double exhibition, such cheap drama, totally unnecessary. The makeup man standing over her chair checked his work and approved of the exact duplication of the makeup she had used for the pose, allowing, however for the artificial lights which would now be used at the unveiling. The basic fine bones had made his work easy. He could be a happier man if all his clients had such good basics.

Outside, the evening moved serenely, even triumphantly forward. Stimulated by the New York experience, Silva was at his best. He had rarely enjoyed any of his openings as he was now doing. The press of unfamiliar notables he handled well. There were other famous artists present whose work he knew and liked. Also there were the beautiful women, some of whom were foreign nobility he had known before in Europe. There were others whom he wished he had known and someday might make arrangements to know. I love New York, he sang silently, exactly as he had heard the refrain on the radio. Sipping champagne, he blessed Miss

Bennett or Gail Blake or whoever she was, for being the catalyst of all this glory.

Much later, the musicians played an impressive fanfare. Conversation halted as everyone slowly turned to the raised area curtained in velvet. The lights on the periphery lowered as those in the center intensified. Then came the slow opening of the curtains and there before them was revealed La Dama de Lila immortalized on canvas, and below, exactly posed and dressed, was the original model. As one, the crowd gasped and half a moment of silence followed. It was almost eerie, for the impact of the painting was doubled by the presence of the model.

Benton, who had almost worked his way through the crowd to Silva stopped, immobilized by the sight of her and in this setting. Neither he nor Clem had had any idea she would appear with the painting. They had only thought to contact the Maestro. Finally a collective murmur rose then broke into a crescendo of applause. On all sides came exclamations of approval and congratulations were showered on Silva who accepted them with modest nods and sotto-voce thanks. The applause diminished and rose again to die away in the hum of excited comments.

Gail Blake kept her pose, muscles falling into the old familiar pattern until the curtain slowly closed. When it opened again, she was gone -- to Benton's dismay and to Anthony and John's amazement and chagrin.

Conversation even more animated rose to correspond with the champagne which was being even more copiously served. Position near the picture was maneuvered by groups although its visibility was clear throughout the room.

Benton and Clem got to Silva within seconds, not an easy job at this time, and offered congratulations.

Silva, now almost euphoric, greeted them with he Spanish abrazo: "I'm happy to see you," he exclaimed raising his voice above the din, "Most happy. Now we can clear up that little misunderstanding."

"We would love to, Maestro," Benton replied not daring to hope.

"Maybe we could all celebrate a little, privately at your place later, Maestro," Clem suggested.

"Of course, of course!" Silva replied patting their backs. "Just wait for me. I'll be going home in an hour or so. Just wait."

"We will, we will!" they chorused.

In another part of the room, John whispered to Anthony, "It was her? She's something! Got class -- for sure! You're certain she's your gun?"

"Look, I've hired her. Sometimes tracked her. It's her all right!"

At the other end of the room near the Maestro, Benton and Clem felt the surge of success achieved. "God! What a windfall!" Benton said, "Let's hang around him."

"Don't worry!" Clem replied smiling. "Maybe this'll be the solution. You stay here with him. I'm going to check to see if she's still here, or find out if we can reach her."

"O.K. I'll be wherever he is."

Clem's quest was in vain, which did not surprise him. She was gone, and all inquiries arrived at a dead end. The museum staff referred him to Pelayo who was no help at all. He greeted him warmly, but excused himself with equal grace after denying any knowledge of the model's whereabouts. The Maestro was their only hope to reach Miss Bennett.

Now, another fanfare came, rolling over the group, taking them by surprise. Silva was on the platform in front of a microphone, smiling and waiting for complete silence. He spoke in Spanish which was simultaneously translated by one of the museum staff at another microphone. Thanking the public for the warm reception of his latest work, he paused dramatically and warned that he was going to enter another area, one which he should never have entered in the first place. The crowd was now completely hushed, anticipating an extremely important announcement. It came. He explained that politics should be forbidden to an artist such as he. He even evoked a ripple of laughter to lighten the moment. Then came the crux of the speech. He renounced Communism, explaining all of his reasons concisely and at the end, admitting that his stubborn nature had delayed his confession too long.

A surprised public at first was at a loss, but quickly recovered with hearty applause. There were even some cries of "bravo" and "olé".

It was quite late when Silva and Pelayo could take their leave, for reporters had surrounded Silva, getting even more of his reasons which he expounded at length with the help of the same interpreter.

Standing by, vastly relieved and as surprised as the rest, Benton and Clem felt they had run the traditional gamut of emotions. First there had been Silva's warm reception of them, his willingness to invite them to "straighten out misunderstandings." Then had come the unexpected appearance of Gail Blake, and now this lucid, calm and logical renunciation of a political position for which he had been well known. It had at times overshadowed even his fame as an artist. What more could there possibly be for one evening? They now felt completely confident that Silva would be safe under these circumstances.

They were mistaken. Anthony and John, of whose presence they were unaware, knew nothing of the reasons for the contract against the life of the artist. They did, however know of their financial necessities and the sight of Silva reinforced their determination to complete the arrangement. It would be easier, they knew, to recognize him, now that they had seen him in the flesh. They left the museum with a feeling of accomplishment, having now identified their target.

Gail Blake had previously arranged her departure through one of the service doors. A waiting rented limousine and driver whisked her home within ten minutes, for wanting to insure her privacy and the bother of midtown traffic, she avoided the bother of taking her own car.

Once home, she quickly shed her famous dress, then the lingerie, and relaxed in a tub filled with foam until she felt completely rid of the museum and the picture. Then later she sank into bed in the foam of a sea green nightgown, and sank back against the pillows, glad she had finished with her nerve-wracking chore. The radio played softly as she selected a novel from the night table.

An hour later, the late news program carried the Paco Silva renunciation of Communism, and she realized he had kept his promise. Whether it would save his life or not was now up to her. However, having decided to savor the moment, brief though it might be, she changed the novel for a fashion magazine and engrossed herself in a preview of the Parisian fall collections.

Later, she heard Silva and Pelayo enter and reached for her robe, wanting to share their success and be congratulated for her part in it. She walked into the living room and halted in surprise to see they had brought Benton and Clem. They too stared unbelievingly at her. It would have been hard to determine who was most astonished.

Silva broke the moment of startled silence moving forward to lead her to a chair. "My dear friend, my hostess, my best model!" he exclaimed. "Here she is! And here we are! Now we can relax and all be friends!"

She looked unbelievingly at him and then at Benton. Silva disappeared into the kitchen where he began to make a fuss looking for a tray, glasses and the right chilled bottle. Pelayo laughed uncomfortably and gestured the other two to be seated. Silva returned with the champagne which Pelayo was happy to help him serve. The total embarrassment was partially covered as they accepted their glasses.

"Very good to see you again," Benton said to her in the manner of any casual acquaintance.

"Rather a surprise," she managed to answer while being forced to accept her glass.

The electricity in the air did not escape Silva. "Now Gail," he said, "it's time we all understood everything. These men, like you, were trying to help me -- just doing their job!"

She stared coolly at him and took a very small sip of champagne.

"Please forgive us. I can see we're intruding. But it's just that we wanted to clear up a few points." Benton accepted a glass from Pelayo who, like Silva was assiduously trying to smooth over the moment.

Then suddenly all began to speak at once, then stopped. Silva's voice rose again as he, taking the role of host, and still full of his success, began to pass some hors d'oeuvres he had garnered from the kitchen. He began to go over the events in Mexico and explained his baseless fear of Benton. Then came the justification of their flight to New York.

Although she did not look at him, Benton clearly felt her discomfort. While nodding sagely as Silva, aided by Pelayo, made his explanations and rationalizations, he was acutely aware of her antagonism. Aided by all the champagne of the evening, Silva was now at his best. His euphoria mounted as he explained, joked, turned his wit against himself occasionally, and frankly admitted that he knew so little about politics, neither Capitalism, or Socialism, or Communism, and that all the years he had defended Communism had been simply a ploy to get him even more noticed and to prove his versatility - the painter- politician! He made much of these two words, never dreaming how it set Gail Blake's teeth on edge, and made Benton and Clem nervous. This had been the crux of all the trouble. The problem Silva now so lightly passed off humorously had been deadly serious not too long before, and now, as Gail Blake reflected, for her it was still of the essence.

The atmosphere could not help but mellow with Silva as he was. It was difficult to resist him. She realized why his coterie of intelligent talented people circulated around him in whichever country he happened to be. She sat, still tense with her mind swiftly turning. So he had found her. Now it was another factor to be reckoned with. If Anthony did not liquidate her first, this man had plans in one way or another to undo her -- to cause her undoing. She must act before Anthony got Silva. There he sat as though at some tea party sipping champagne and nibbling at those curled-up dry hors d'oeuvres she had meant to give to the cat if even she would eat them.

Emily meanwhile had jumped in Pelayo's lap and was sound asleep, surfeited with food and attention, never realizing that she was helping to calm the group's nerves by her completely relaxed body and almost inaudible purring.

An hour passed filled with an amazing performance by Silva baked by Pelayo. Without realizing it he had involved everyone in animated conversation, almost winning over Gail Blake in spite of herself. The evening at the museum was reprised, prior events in Mexico also. Silva's renunciation was examined, explored and congratulated. At last, Benton rose and Clem followed suit.

"We must be getting along," Benton smiled. "It's really late and all of you have got to be tired."

"Don't go yet," Silva begged, reluctant for the night to end.

However, they prevailed and took their leave, Pelayo seeing them to the door. As Benton passed her he paused to ask if he could make an appointment to see her the next day. She had expected this and quickly nodded, determined to risk a final showdown.

"Shall I pick you up around eight?" he asked.

"That will be fine," she replied with a smile to prove that she too could be urbane.

After their departure, an embarrassed silence ensued, and she silently rose and went into her room.

"I warned you, Maestro," Pelayo said when she had left. "Now she's mad."

Silva shook his head. "Well, I don't care. She needs to see more people! What kind of a life does she have? That solitary lonesome woman! Wearing those beautiful clothes for nobody's eyes -- playing that beautiful music for nobody's ears!"

"Only us. And, of course the cat!" agreed Pelayo.

"Exactly. And when we leave it will be just the cat!"

"Yes, but are we the ones to change the course of her life?"

"Well, she tried to save me, didn't she?" Silva riposted as they finished their glasses and headed rather unsteadily to their respective rooms. "And now I am going to save her from herself!" he threw back at Pelayo just before shutting his door.

CHAPTER 18

The newspapers the next day amply covered the preview of the latest Silva, hailed by the critics as one of his masterpieces. Pelayo contentedly retired behind a pile, garnering articles which he arranged for the Maestro to read directly. Pictures appeared, some with Gail Blake, others without her. Forced to look by an enthusiastic Pelayo, she more than ever regretted her participation. She was mentioned as the mysterious model, Lady Lilac or Lady X who had disappeared so suddenly. More than one columnist speculated on her identity. As she read on, she felt a rising apprehension. Why had she ever involved herself? The very last thing she needed at this moment was any kind of fame or notoriety.

She pretended an enthusiasm she did not feel, trying to match Pelayo's. The Maestro, although enormously pleased, maintained a becoming reserve, but it was noticed that his time at his easel was done in short spurts, punctuated with frequent glasses of brandy.

"There is nothing in this world like the morning after," he commented during lunch, "mixed with a million memories."

"And what about all those invitations?" Pelayo asked. "I told them I would contact them later after speaking to you."

"Tomorrow -- tomorrow!" he declared. "Today just let me get my head back together!"

As evening approached, Gail Blake recognized the familiar and unwelcome feeling of unpreparedness before an important examination. She hated herself for putting him in the role of her most difficult professor, but there seemed to be no help for it. As she dressed, she decided to let him do the talking, ask the questions to which she had already thought of evasive answers, and to leave the ball in his court at all times. She selected a simple dress, navy blue' nothing to adorn it but a long necklace of semiprecious transparent beads which she had bought on the beach in Acapulco years ago, but which she loved and considered a good luck charm.

Silva and Pelayo had elected to stay home and rest in spite of the flood of invitations and newly initiated telephone calls which Pelayo managed.

As she verified their plans, she realized that she was indeed being the housemother.

Benton picked her up and as they left the building heading for his car he asked if she had a preference for a place to have an hour or so of conversation.

"Anywhere will do," she replied, remembering her resolutions.

He took the river drive ringing Manhattan, occasionally filling in the silence telling her how much he missed the response of his corvette in contrast to his present rented car. Still she noted what a good driver he was in the heavy traffic of the drive, but remained silent beyond one or two monosyllabic responses.

Off base ever since the museum opening, Benton still felt disoriented by her unexpected appearance beneath the picture and in her own apartment with Silva and Pelayo who seemed to be perfectly at ease there. Suddenly he decided to make a daring move. Reaching the entrance to the George Washington Bridge, he turned and headed across, continuing until taking the Englewood exit.

He pulled up in front of the door to her home. She had still maintained silence.

"Shall we go in?" he asked as he cut the motor.

"If you like," she stoically replied.

They went to the entrance where they paused, the moment tense between them. Finally he reached for the key had had made and opened the door. As they entered, she automatically switched on the lights.

"You realize you are guilty of breaking and entering my house," she said after looking around and finally choosing a position on the couch in the small living room.

"I realize everything I have done," he replied, taking a chair.

"And just what do you want of me? You come here; enter my house after harassing me in Mexico -- following me, hounding me, and in general making my life miserable. Now I see you've invaded my privacy even here!"

He did not answer.

"I want you to know," she continued more forcefully, "that I resent it! I'm going to complain!"

"And to whom?" he asked with a smile.

They exchanged silent stares for a moment.

"Now let's begin again," he finally said settling back, "and why not from the very beginning."

She made no comment and reached in her bag for a cigarette, having foresightedly brought it to use as a prop. She lit it before he could show gallantry. At this time she was fighting back a threatened headache which she feared presaged a migraine attack.

"You were Gail Blake, music teacher, wife and mother. Husband a captain in the Marines," he paused for her reaction, watched as she blew a cloud of smoke which seemed to make a protective barrier for her.

"His tragic death in Lebanon naturally had terrible repercussions for you." He glanced at the mantle above the fireplace which held the picture of a uniformed man framed in silver. "You devoted yourself to your daughter," he continued. This brought a quick movement and a quicker recovery. "She was a brilliant girl, academically and musically. She might have become a professional -- concert..."

"Never!" she exploded to his surprise.

"Oh?"

She did not answer, now in the full grip of a pounding headache combined with a dawning helpless rage.

"A few years ago, this daughter was tragically killed -- forgive me, but I have to say all this..." he interrupted himself, but seeing no response he continued. "Shortly thereafter, Mrs. Gail Blake disappeared only to come back for brief interludes, calling the neighbors to ask for the girl. This always happened around five or six and in winter."

She had stiffened, refusing to meet his glance or to show her pain.

"Meanwhile there appeared in a New York penthouse owned by Gail Blake a woman calling herself Heather Bennett. She lived in this place bought years ago by Gail Stewart -- your maiden name, I believe."

How quickly he had researched the penthouse history, she thought. In less than twenty-four hours he had gotten this data. What means he must have at his disposal for such efficiency.

"In other words, a very young Gail Stewart married a John Blake, hence Gail Blake. Heather Bennett is your -- your 'nom de guerre?'"

She was now in the full grip of her headache, but she stared in his direction. "I want to know," she finally spoke, "what right you have to invade my home, my privacy, to bring up my tragedies, parade them before me -- you come here to taunt me with it all -- just who are you anyway? Do you or don't you have a search warrant. What do you want from me?"

"I'll soon have the answer to all of that," he answered, "but I want you to understand that I know what you are now -- and what you were in Cuernavaca -- what your purpose was -- your assignment."

"I don't need to account to you in any way, Mr. Benton. You're supposed to be a journalist anyway. Not a policeman."

"I am a journalist. I write for travel publications."

"Then why this curiosity about me -- my affairs? You've been to an awful lot of trouble for just a simple interview."

They were at a stalemate for the moment. With all the information collected, he remained unsatisfied, trying to put the pieces together and always ending up with some of the most important ones missing. Several of his guesses had ended up a blind alley. In some way she remained almost as untouchable as he had found her. Only the memory of that one night dining and dancing made her seem human and even then, he suspected she had harbored an ulterior motive. She was devious, unpredictable, lethal, tragic and most of all, indefinable.

She looked at him in the half-light and her mind skipped back to the years of her marriage -- for he still used the fragrance of the small Paris shop, inviting the memory.

Her pain and rage began to subside and she almost regretted that he was out to destroy her, for she now realized that he was the first and only person to elicit any sort of inner response from her in this, her second incarnation. Though he had triggered anger and exasperation, still he had managed to penetrate her defense against more hurt, and she suddenly hated him the more for that.

"So where are we now?" he asked.

"It's your interview," she reminded him, suspecting his feeling of impending defeat. Then urged by a sudden desire to confuse him further, she extinguished her smoldering cigarette, went to a picture near the mantle which hid a small wall safe, maneuvered the combination and drew out a large square envelope.

"Here's something you missed. Read what's there." She offered it to him.

He slowly opened it and drew out several plastically preserved copies of newspaper clippings. To his surprise he read of a ten-year-old child, a Gail Stewart, surprising music critics of major cities in the United States and Europe with her genius at the piano, her instinct for phrasing, modulating, for executing the most difficult music with understanding. He looked up at her in amazement.

"But this was you?"

"One and the same," she answered enjoying his reaction.

He returned to the articles, carefully replacing each sheet on finishing. "I seem to remember reading something about this child," he murmured. At last he finished, but not before noting one or two veiled warnings by critics who had praised her work. Was she being pushed too fast? Too hard? What about her life as a ten-year-old?

She watched him, amused. Had she but known, he was not only disconcerted, but also deeply disturbed.

"Look, level with me -- tell me what happened. First a child prodigy, then the modest housewife, then the change of name and the luxury penthouse. What the hell was happening? I don't get it!"

Savoring his capitulation, she prolonged the moment by taking another cigarette, this time permitting him to light it.

"It's there -- all there," she finally replied. "That warning to my parents, pushing me, exploiting me -- no child should be subjected to that sort of thing. And the terrible secret -- theirs and mine -- was that I was playing these classics entirely by ear. It went on until I was thirteen."

"Burnout?"

"And more. A complete breakdown, lasting a year where I'd scream if I even saw a piano. I was in a Swiss sanitarium where they prohibited my parents from seeing me -- especially my parents."

"Where are they now?"

"Killed in a plane accident -- one of the mountains too high where they lived to be near me. They were a stage couple, playing minor circuits. Both were good on piano -- both could dance, and they formed a rather good act, as I remember."

"And you?"

"When they saw I had the knack, with perfect memory, perfect pitch, they stopped to dedicate themselves to me. I was their path to real fame."

He digested this, remembering the pictures he had just seen. The little girl, hair carefully curled, the ribbon bow, the organdy flounces, white shoes and socks -- the prodigy capable of amazing the public and critics -- at what cost?

"And then what happened?"

Now she felt like Sherazade, telling the story that would delay her doom. She had never really intended to launch upon it, yet, once started, she capitulated to the luxury of recounting all of it to another -- something she had never done before. Lured on, she spoke almost automatically, dealing with Gail Stewart or Gail Blake as though with a third person.

"A guardian was appointed for me by the Court. The money I earned was reserved and invested until I reached my majority. The penthouse was one of the investments, by the way. I had been shepherded through enough education to qualify for the conservatory. So even though married, I finished. Now I'm a real musician, thank God. That means a lot to me."

"And thank God for the laws protecting child performers."

"Oh, yes!"

"But you married and lived in this modest way?"

She laughed. "You might not understand this, but when I married, frankly I was looking for a nice bourgeois life with cottage, baby, car, exactly like some of the sitcoms I watched on TV. Furthermore my husband was a Marine -- a Marine with principle. He refused to use my money. We lived on his salary and what I earned as a music teacher at home. My invested money was put aside for Terry to use when she grew up."

It took him a moment or two to digest this. She returned the clippings to the safe.

"And then the tragedy of your husband, and later your daughter."

She flinched and looked away. For the first time he was sure of his ground. He waited. "You went into another business after the death of Terry -- because of Terry, perhaps."

It was too much. She stood and began pacing. It began to surge, then to spill over.

"Yes! Yes! Every time I did it I..."

"You pretended it was her murderer."

"How did you know?" She was taken aback and struggled for control.

He watched her, still waiting, and saw her realization that she had given herself away. Yet he had no sense of victory.

"To get even?" he persisted?

"To get even," she repeated, sitting and meeting his gaze. "And I wanted to send a message to the gods up there too."

"Who had taken everything away from you?"

"Yes! But in such a way! That tragedy in Iran -- those Marines -- that could have been avoided had they been on higher ground -- it was avoidable! And Terry -- there was absolutely no need for her to take that shortcut! I had warned her about it so many times -- it was avoidable! So it all seemed a plot -- a plot against me!" She held back unaccustomed tears, hoping not to break down in front of him of all people. Now she was practically at his mercy. Somehow she had ceased to care.

"They never found the killer, I understand."

"No." Her tone was accusing and he caught it immediately.

He represented the law -- all law -- and it had failed her. <u>He</u> had failed her.

"You realize he probably has been caught?"

"You mean later? For another crime?"

"Yes. I can quote you percentages."

"Never mind percentages."

In the silence which again stretched between them, her headache ceased and her feeling of relief made her wonder if penitents felt that way after confession. He had drawn back part of the curtain. Now he was going to see it all, she decided. She still felt the strong urge to shock him, to surprise him.

"And you come back here to pretend she's coming home from school?"

"To pretend she's coming home from school. Yes."

"It makes you happy?"

"Yes, for a while."

Again he took stock of the woman sitting there. Who would have known how completely lost, tragic and emotionless a creature had evolved from what had happened to her.

"But now you're protecting Silva," he continued. "I don't understand your turnaround."

"Something happened when I looked at Silva's picture of me. He had painted me as I was and as I am now, and the change must have brought me to my senses. I don't really know. It was like awakening from a bad dream. I came out of it."

"In Mexico?"

"Yes."

"Then why did you run away? We were on the same side after your conversion."

She gave a short laugh. "Silva still didn't trust you. I used this to help shake you from my heels. I realized you were out to get me. So to protect myself, I took him into hiding to my New York place where supposedly you couldn't find either him or me."

"Well, well, well," he mused, trying to fathom her thinking.

"You people bungle a lot. Right now, for instance, you think your job's done, right?"

"Well, Silva's alive and well, the plot was foiled, the 'villain's' known. And the serendipity came about as they delved into the dealings of 'Gentleman Joe'. Then as luck would have it, the lieutenant, Pasquel Donato turned State's evidence."

"You people still have so much to learn." Her attitude presaged unfinished business. When would he ever fathom the whole story? And why did he want to?

"Look, I was responsible for Silva in Mexico, and if anything's pending,

I still feel responsible. Don't get any ideas about my job!"

"Yes, I knew you for Government right away. You've finished with your assignment down there, but you want another citation right? And I'm your stepping stone."

"That's your theory?"

"And I refuse the honor. I prefer to die in my bed."

Although more was falling into place, he still lacked the key. She was close to the truth of his assignment, but new factors had now entered. He kept silent.

She rose and started a record on the small stereo at the side of the upright. Grieg flowed into the room. The magic of it overlaid the turbulence. She turned for the dining room buffet and prepared two drinks.

"Over ice," she said offering him one.

"Yes, my New York drink. Thanks."

Raising the glasses slightly relieved the awkwardness, and the music distracted. Resting her glass, she went to the piano to join in a part of it.

He leaned back and closed his eyes. The tangled web. He considered it carefully and began to probe his own work. Wasn't most of it based on deception? How often had he killed? But of course wasn't that different? Or was it? He had received three commendations. The concerto ended.

"Who's the pianist on the record?" he asked.

"Little me at age twelve," she answered. "I always meant to transfer it to a CD. What you just heard was a duet with the then Gail Stewart and the now Gail Blake."

He could think of nothing to say for a moment. Then, "You were really something -- I'm rather dazzled."

"Thank you," she answered, casting a housewife's eyes over the room. She straightened the picture covering the safe and quickly rinsed the glasses in the kitchen. She returned, her air of dismissal evident. "I'm ready if you've finished your 'interview'."

She extinguished the lights, and followed him to the door, which she locked with care.

CHAPTER 19

Benton stormed into the hotel suite awakening Clem from a sound sleep. Even for them it was late.

"Damn, damn, damn!" he exploded, switching on the light.

Clem sat up blinking, but immediately awake from long habit. He was accustomed to Benton's moments of frustration, and silently settled back to listen.

"What the hell am I to do -- are we to do?" he amended. "She makes me furious, and believe me, she's sick, sick, sick!"

"Doesn't surprise me at all. Got a cigarette? Might as well be comfortable."

Benton tossed him a pack and sprawled in a chair. "I took her to her Englewood place and she never raised a hair. She put me on the defensive. Get that!"

"Did you face her with what we know?"

"Yes, and in so many words she admitted it."

"No firm yes or no?"

"It was pretty clear what she is."

"Then what's the next step?"

"Well, it seems Silva might still be a target. She implied that." He rose to grab a cigarette from the pack he had thrown, oblivious to his determination to quit smoking. Carrying the pack had been simply a test. Now he really needed one. "And it just might be she's out to play a lone hand."

"I thought she said she wasn't sick anymore," Clem asked.

"Oh, damnit, I don't know what the hell she is -- you figure it out."

"Well, if you remember, old buddy, this was our little sideline project -- now it's all gotten to you, seems like."

"Well it's all so damn frustrating! I'm just trying to tie up what we did down there. If Silva is still up for a hit, that would cancel out the grateful thanks from headquarters -- right?"

"You can just bet!"

"So that more or less makes it official -- morally, I mean, for us. Silva's got to be guarded. And she knows more than she's telling!"

"I hear you!"

"I'm putting a tail on her and a guard on Silva."

"But I get the idea he paints all day on the terrace up there."

"Yeah, but he and that secretary go out for walks and it would only take a minute -- and after all that publicity about the new picture!"

"No problem. Headquarters will ante up!"

"O.K., gotta bring them in again."

Clem took another cigarette and opted for a chair. It looked like a long night. "Now clue me in. What happened to hex you so much tonight?"

"I can't just put a tag on it. First off, that woman was a child prodigy on piano."

"You don't say!"

Benton outlined the story to Clem; stopping only to call headquarters, then to fix a nightcap for them both. An hour later, he left for his own room trying to ignore Clem's knowing smile and quelling a strong urge to punch him in the nose for it. He went to bed and tossed and hour before sinking into a light slumber filled with strange dreams.

On the other hand, Miss Bennett, known now as Gail Blake, felt liberated. She tried to tell herself that she had compounded her problems, that she had left herself vulnerable to prosecution, that she had betrayed herself to Government -- to Law itself, but she could not bring herself to worry.

After checking to see if Silva and Pelayo had safely retired, again feeling the den mother in so doing, she prepared for bed, chose a shimmering flowered chiffon gown, and with neither tapes nor book nor champagne, settled down, dimmed the light and slept as she had rarely slept since childhood.

There was good luck for her the next morning. The long-coveted address had finally appeared in the Times, included in a story about the family of "Gentleman Joe" where Anthony was interviewed denying his father's guilt. This was in the face of recent revelations of his father's involvement in trucking, waterfront and union activities in a questionable manner. The second in command, hoping for a much lighter sentence, had revealed so much the prosecutors were having their work made much easier. The only face not mentioned in the litany was Anthony's "sideline," and that was really because the lieutenant knew nothing about it.

Gail Blake noted that Anthony stoutly defended his father to the press, making sure his weeping mother was present to underline the "injustice" of it all. But what interested her most was the address in Long Island of her target -- Anthony. No more stalking in vain in front of the Courthouse. Neither more heavy cameras nor exaggerated sports outfits. If she could work it out before Gregory Benton's move against her, she would be content, for in the full light of morning, she was more than ever sure there would be such a move. Those government people always wanted another feather in their caps. Meanwhile she enjoyed her newly found peace of mind.

Carefully memorizing the address, she dropped the paper and practiced piano for an hour. It was a beautiful Saturday. Pelayo was out on his daily walk. Silva, slowly unwinding from his triumph was on another part of the terrace painting as usual. He had returned to his routine, refusing invitations, dedicating himself to his "New York period."

Emily, the cat, was grooming herself on her favorite sofa, stopping occasionally to rest and to listen. She considered the household a serene one, worthy of her. The music was playing softly, the way a cat most liked; the people were going about their business in a casual, pleasant manner, and they were all cat people with friendly laps and no sudden movements to annoy her during her frequent naps. Life was good.

Pelayo, at the museum noted the crowds still in front of the "Dama de Lila." He was also negotiating with several prospective buyers, including the museum itself. In short, he was in his element. Besides, he, having now finished the Egyptology and French Impressionist wings, had begun to dedicate himself to visiting the period rooms which he felt few visitors appreciated. As he bustled out after breakfast, pince-nez in place, suit impeccable, he took on the patina of an old-fashioned New York executive, headed for his office, as indeed the museum had become for him.

Gail Blake did not hear from Gregory Benton, yet strangely enough felt no pressure or apprehension. She seemed to be in some strange dimension where sound, dreamless sleep was hers together with an unaccustomed well being. She told herself that all this would disappear at the least propitious moment any day now. Law and Order in capital letters would appear and consummate her humiliation. One piece of unfinished business remained -- Anthony Scavoni. If there could be anything to salvage of her life so studded with tragedy, she now pinned her hopes on making the world safe for Francisco Silva. She reasoned that this gesture would be her expiation.

At dinner that evening, she joined in all the bonhomie generated by her two guests. Pelayo had his saga of who wanted the picture and for how much. He seemed to be playing private buyers against the museum, for other museums had sent emissaries. Silva beamed, assuming his mantel of modesty. The table silver gleamed in the dimmed light, and the day's roses were still in bud in a glorious arrangement on the buffet. The building restaurant, delivering daily, had outdone itself with the menu -- this time it was Japanese cuisine as a change from the predominantly French masterpieces usually sent in.

They took turns with toasts, and Silva gallantly referred to the "new Gail Blake" as an important change from Mrs. Duran and Miss Heather Bennett.

"It is mainly in the eyes," he emphasized. "As a painter, I noted the eyes immediately. Then you seem different in other respect too. At this moment I cannot exactly place it."

"I'm sleeping better," she answered, "and that means everything."

CHAPTER 20

More than two weeks had passed since the first showing of the new Paco Silva painting at the Metropolitan Museum of Art, and Mr. Gerard was far from happy. In the first place, few had believed him when he mentioned that he was the couturier of the simple but striking summer dress worn by the model. He had made discreet announcements to various guests encountered at the opening, but had definitely not received the affection he felt he deserved. Finally he had tried, as others had done, to trace the model to her home, only to find that after several years of service as her coiffeur, he not only was ignorant of her address, but knew practically nothing about her. She had come to have her hair coiffed, had chatted with him about hairstyles and dress fashions, paid and tipped him well, and had departed with a small smile. His admiration of her clothes -- obviously high fashion -- had inspired him to create her lilac dress, which had been immortalized by an internationally famous artist.

"You should call a press conference," his housemate had advised the day after the showing. "You got practically no credit at all!" This was sincerely said, even though there had been a slight reserve between them caused by his obvious tendency at times to show an almost overpowering envy.

"You really think so?" asked Mr. Gerard, his hopes rising.

"Of course! Just what would the whole thing have amounted to without that dress!

As a matter of fact, I really think you should change over to fashion!"

"Perhaps I will after all," replied Mr. Gerard. "But what a hell of a thing! That bitch never mentioned my name!"

"But she never spoke at all," his friend pointed out. "And she did send an invitation."

"Well somebody should have mentioned something about my dress. Nobody there seemed to care about it!"

"I thought you had the addresses of all your customers."

"Now why would I do that? They come to me! And if my secretary can work them into my schedule at the salon, I will do them! Of course, I never do the washing, just give the design to my assistant for the curlers, then I do the styling -- the coiffure!"

"I know all that, but what I think now is you should call the press, dummy!"

"And what must I say? Mr. Know-it-all?"

"Well, tell them you know that model they're all talking about and she's a customer for whom you did the favor of designing and making that dress. That could get you off the ground as a couturier. Any child could see that!"

"Well why don't you see about it then, since you know so much?" Mr. Gerard suggested as he finished dressing and sprayed his own teased coiffure. This he said casually to hide his ignorance and therefore slight shyness in such matters. His friend, being a chorus boy, second from left in one of the hit Broadway shows, would really know more about such things.

Thus challenged, certain calls were made to various fashion columnists on the many magazines and journals issued from the New York base. Mr. Gerard was ecstatic, visualizing the group assembled in his Madison Avenue shop with its gold-mirrored walls, the gold spangled accoutrements, down to the combs and brushes. The haughty male assistants had been chosen not only for their efficiency, but also for their striking good looks. There was Mr. Adrian, Mr. Andre, Mr. Emile, and Mr. Xavier, formerly known to their mothers respectively as Abe, Andy, Emilio, and Jack, none of whom deigned to wear a protective apron and worked under Mr. Gerard's direction in their Armani suits.

Within a week, it was all arranged. White wine was placed on an improvised bar alongside the caterer's Danish hors d'oeuvres. The ever-impeccable assistants were at the ready to attend Mr. Gerard's guests. Mr. Gerard himself was resplendent in a gleaming white sheen gabardine suit, a cloth popularized in Hollywood, now enjoying a resurgence. A ruffled shirt and white Italian silk tie and gold cufflinks were his accessories.

Assuming a <u>sang froid</u> he was far from feeling, Mr. Gerard leaned against the receptionist's counter in an attitude of faint disdain for all and sundry. He smoked a gold cigarette drawn from its flat gold case, and watched Arlyn as he bustled about giving unnecessary directions to the hired bartender and the two waiters who were only one step from telling him what he could do and where he could go. Chic customers with legitimate previous appointments innocently entered and were hastily dealt with, finding themselves outside in no time at all.

Two photographers wandered in, heavily laden with their paraphernalia.

"Where is she?" they demanded.

Mr. Gerard stepped forward. "Welcome gentlemen!" he began as Arlyn joined them.

"Where's the lilac dame?" repeated the gentlemen of the press.

Mr. Gerard turned to Arlyn. "Did you tell them she would be here?"

"Of course I did! How else would anyone come?" he answered sotto voce.

"She's been detained," Arlyn smiled broadly. "You know women! Meanwhile, let me show you the facsimile of the dress she wore -- designed and executed by my friend, Gerard Delacey."

The photographers turned and viewed the dress without much enthusiasm, but snapped two pictures. Meanwhile three reporters entered, all of whom asked the same question to be answered the same way. They were ushered to the refreshment table and dub in, inasmuch as it was almost lunchtime, after which they showed signs of impatience as Mr. Gerard explained how he was inspired to create the dress worn by a Ms. Bennett. "Well, could you give us her address -- just who is she?" were some of the demands. In spite of their suavity, the excellence of the repast, and the vintage of the wines, the busy reporters and photographers wandered out to other assignments. This pattern continued for two hours more during which there was no actual assembly of the fourth estate ever in attendance. Their homing instinct clearly pointed to a certain Mr. Gerard of whose prototype there were many in New York, who either knew nothing of the "Lilac Dame" or chose not to tell, who was seizing the main chance to promote his overdone salon and himself. By three in the afternoon, the place contained only the staff, a depleted table and empty wine bottles. Mr. Gerard retired to the men's room, emerged half an hour later red-eyed and exuding hauteur. He gave Arlyn a withering look, passed through the front door without a word, and went down to one of his favored places in the Village where he proceeded to drown his sorrows.

But all was not lost. The following week, one of the specialized weeklies following the antics of the rich and famous and usually inventing some for them, came out with a flattering picture of Mr. Gerard holding the lilac dress and declaring in the headlines, "This famous dress cost only five dollars to make!!"

When he was triumphantly shown this single denigrating piece of publicity garnered by Arlyn who had so assiduously arranged it, Mr. Gerard proceeded to throw his friend's expensive wardrobe out of the apartment into the hallway, almost causing him to be late for his show that night.

CHAPTER 21

The day had been rainy, but by evening the rain had stopped, leaving the night pavements of Manhattan gleaming beneath the street lamps, reflecting the changing green and red traffic lights. Gail Blake decided it was time to make her move. Changing into black pants and matching jacket, she topped it with a black beret. In five minutes she had taken leave of the two men ensconced in deep armchairs in front of the Spanish TV programs, and in another ten she had taken her car from the basement garage of her building.

Heading toward the Long Island Expressway, she maneuvered the traffic easily until arriving at the neighborhood she sought.

The reduced street lighting in the suburbs made identification difficult, especially since trees hid many of the house numbers and an occasional house was so recessed as to be invisible behind hedges and shrubs. Finally she made the identification, noting that the Scavoni grounds extended into the street behind the house. Much of the terrain presented a homogenous expanse of lawn shared by several families, not having been fenced off. However, in the dark, lit only by a few tentative stars, she caught sight of the form of a series of grape arbors, stretching several yards long, with tables and chairs. A small garden, presumably of vegetables, lay to the side. Instinct directed her, helped by the mention of the grape vines in the press.

Parking the car some distance away, she walked slowly back, hoping the dog leash law held true in this area. She was lucky to encounter no one enjoying their expanse of ground, due, no doubt, to the dampness from the recent rains.

Stalking had always been a matter of playing it by ear for her, a waiting game to be done with patience, but yet with the reflexes at the ready in case the golden chance suddenly appeared. From the safety of the vines, she checked the back entrance and noted lights in the windows and shadows passing back and forth. She was surprised at the modest proportions of the house.

The outlines of the shadow figure suggested a woman working in her kitchen. A tedious hour passed during which it became obvious that Anthony was not at home and would probably not be at home for some time. She weighed watching and waiting longer, longing for the opportunity to intercept him as he arrived to park his car. Meanwhile she sat and ate some of the ripening grapes, listening for the sound of an arriving motor. Another hour passed, and she made the decision to leave and return the following night on the theory that Anthony might not delay his return two nights in succession -- a random guess, but her boredom won out.

She drove back to the city, entered the parking area below the building and noticed a dimmer lighting. Only by long usage was she able to find her allotted space. The elevator was nearby and as she approached it, some instinct made her wary. The figure beside it spoke.

"Well, hello, stranger."

She recognized Anthony's voice.

"Hello," she said pausing. He was blocking the path to the elevator.

"I've been waiting for you."

"And I've been waiting for you," she answered, judging her distance and space. Her weapon was in her purse, but she was sure he was on the alert for any movement toward it. The hum of the machine started and the door opened. He had obviously timed it, wanting to do the job in her apartment it seemed. Perhaps he planned a two or three-way hit, and upstairs.

"They wouldn't let me in at the door. Wonder why the doorman changed policy?"

"I wonder," she repeated as the doors opened and she was escorted in.

"I notice you changed the locks on your private elevators," he said, assuming the role of an old friend.

"I'm not for hire, if that's what you came for," she said moving away from him as they ascended.

"Now let's see about that," he gave his one sided smile which she was beginning to hate.

Her mind was racing. He wanted to reach her place and kill them all -- even Pelayo, perhaps. Then he could escape through the private elevator stealing her keys. She decided to continue to let him believe she thought he had come on the matter of the earlier job. How ironic they had crossed paths -- she at his house, and he at hers.

"I've been pretty busy lately, going back into music again," she said, maintaining the facade.

"But it doesn't really pay enough, now does it? You like a nice place to live in -- this building, for instance; custom made dresses -- it all adds up, don't forget."

For a moment she wondered if his aim really did concern her re-employment. They ascended rapidly and as the door opened, he stepped back for her to precede him, and she recognized his precaution. As they entered the foyer, she opened her door and turned to him. "Let's talk in this same room as before. Some guests are here, and it's better to be private -- right?"

"Oh, by all means," he exaggerated his politeness and showed interest in some of the apparatus as they entered.

Her relief was mixed with a dilemma. She could possibly draw first in a surprise move, pretending to reach in her bag for a lipstick. Yet she knew she held her home as sacred, and hated any idea of involving her ivory tower in a hit, and least of all in a hit of someone she now thoroughly hated.

The size of the apartment precluded the awareness of Silva and Pelayo of their entry. It was likely that they were either in front of the television or in bed in any case. Anthony meanwhile had made himself comfortable on the seat of the bicycle apparatus, giving her an advantage. He had actually come with the idea of convincing her to do the Silva hit, and later, he planned to deal with her -- thus have her pull his chestnuts from the fire and leaving him with only her to liquidate.

"Now it's hard to believe you've changed your mind about the job," he began reasonably. "I get the feeling somebody might have offered you more money to lay off. I'm onto those deals. Also Paco Silva is living here under your protection. I know that!"

"You're right," she nodded, not surprised at how he equated everything with money. Then another part of her mind asked what would she do with the body if she killed the cretin now. It was one thing to work in a foreign country, sometimes even in a crowded room as she had done in the past, but here, in one's own home, even with the silencer, and with Paco and Pelayo in the apartment. Impossible!

"Well, I tell you what," he was saying. "I'11 give you a bonus. You have a perfect setup here to do the job."

"But I told you..."

"Oh, don't be so silly. Don't give me that lame excuse about the music. You've been paid off! I know the signs. You're no angel, dear lady."

"No devil either, my dear man!"

"What's that supposed to mean?"

"Let's just say by luck I turned out to be an avenging angel -- I noticed that all my assignments amply deserved not to live -- a dictator with years of blood on his hands in Latin America, a defector from your dad's group, who had earned the name of The Exterminator before Hollywood discovered the name -- oh why go on? You know better than I."

"You setting yourself up as some kind of a judge?"

"Not exactly -- only a commentary. Just think of me as 'Angel'."

"You bleeping dames turn me off," he exploded, his urbanity vanishing. "Never saw one yet who was a real pro. Thought you were! I bet you're stuck on this painter guy -- most likely sleeping with him... u he broke off with a short laugh.

In the rage which overwhelmed her she leaped at him in a move often practiced with their martial arts teacher. The hard knife-edge of her hand swept in an arc to the side of his neck. To the carotid artery. Poised precariously as he was against the stationary bicycle, he toppled sideways to the floor, unconscious before he hit it. She had surprised herself with her quick move. She stared down at him, anger subsiding, then bent over him, slapping his cheeks, hoping the impact of his head against the steel supports of the bike had not killed him. How sardonic that earlier she wanted that opportunity, but now she was afraid she had done so. Of course she knew the reason -- her apartment -- not in her apartment.

He slowly recovered, sat up and managed to give her a baffled look. "You'll pay for this," he muttered brokenly, rubbing his neck.

"Not if you pay first," she told him, face close to his. "You low scum! I can kill you so easily -- this minute -- but hate to dirty up my floor with your filthy blood." She pulled his gun from his shoulder holster, and pressed the muzzle against his throat. He cowered.

"You're too vile for me to dirty my rug. How would you like to die in a sack of cement in the river the way your dad likes to do it or in the middle of traffic like his captain explained in court?"

"My dad's innocent!" he gurgled.

It was her turn to laugh. She pressed the muzzle harder. He stopped talking. She realized she was right in estimating his lack of karate as there had been three opportunities for him to get at her within the last five minutes. He moved his head and silently worked his lips. She turned the muzzle to his mouth.

"And watch your nasty mouth from now on with me, you scum, and thank God you're in my place -- otherwise I would kill you and dead!" It all came out now, for as much as she tried to suppress Heather Bennett, the blurred image of her daughter's unknown assailant was forming, and she translated it to the figure now at her mercy.

"Get up," she curtly ordered.

He slowly maneuvered to his feet, clenching his hands and glaring at her. She made another lightening move and kneed him in the groin, immediately doubling him. A minute passed as she stepped back and ordered him to the door.

"Get out, scum! I'll see you later!" She was heedless of consequences as she watched him hobble to the door, and not wanting even his breath to be left she raised a window before he could reach the elevator.

"What the hell have I ever done to you?" he gasped, holding his groin and dragging himself forward, afraid she would again approach him.

"You exist!" she hissed, and pushed him through the elevator door which had opened at that moment.

"You'll pay for this!" he managed to shout behind the door, having gained courage once away from her.

"But you'll pay first!" she rejoined, locking the door and returning to the room where she had left his gun. She stored it on a closet shelf, stretched and relaxed completely by doing a set of exercises taught by her trainer. She examined her fingernails for damage, took a turn on the gym bike, and left the room to check on her guests whom she found had retired.

"Sure, I tailed her O.K. It was mostly easy," the agent reported to Benton.

"How do you mean 'mostly easy'?"

They were in the coffee shop of a midtown hotel, Benton and Clem just back from Washington where they had been given new instructions.

"I mean she stayed in the building till nightfall when I got word from my backup at the garage exit that she was warming up her car. We had to step on it to get to her and with traffic tough too. But we made it and besides, how many Porsches do you see that time of night on the Long Island Expressway?"

"Maybe plenty -- haven't counted."

"She never slowed down till she got to Oak Street and then it got harder. Not much traffic. Hard to keep trailing without her catching on."

"You studied the technique enough to know how by now," Benton threw at him. "Go on." His stomach was tightening. Perhaps he should have stayed in town to handle the thing himself. She might have precipitated events.

"Well she fooled around, cruised around more or less, then parked and went back of Oak Street. She pussyfooted across the lawns till she got to somebody's yard with grape vines, took a seat as comfortable as you please and started eating grapes! Then she went up near the back of the house and peeped in."

"What else?"

"That was it -- but two hours she stayed there!"

Clem laughed. "She must like grapes a lot."

"Well, she just sat there like she was waiting for somebody or something."

"Any cars in the garage?"

"The carport was empty."

"Lights in the house?"

"Yeah."

"Then what?"

"Then she went back to her car, drove back to town -- me following -- and parked it in her garage. And that was that."

"What do you mean, 'that was that'? Didn't you follow her into the garage?"

"What was the use of that? There's an elevator right from there to her apartment."

Benton exploded. "You knuckle-headed son of a bitch! I just wish I could belt you one! You know how many crimes take place in car parks?"

"You hadn't ought to have done that," Clem said, exaggerating his drawl.

"I'm about to report you for this, you dumb bubble-headed cluck! Left her alone!"

"For God's sake, Benton, you never gave me orders to protect her -- to guard her! I was only supposed to be a tail!"

Benton rose, Clem following. "You make me sick," he snarled, turning away. "You're off the job as of now -- get back to local headquarters for reassignment. And don't expect any recommendations from me, either."

They left, leaving an astonished colleague who decided that coffee was not the indicated drink at the moment. He made his way to the bar.

The next morning, Benton telephoned Gail Blake, afterward congratulating himself that he had handled her diplomatically. He spoke in a general way after polite greetings, with the excuse of checking up on Silva, once more repeating that he was responsible for his safety and not to worry about anything.

She garnered that he was biding his time before taking or having her taken in -- just squaring away all loose ends. Her arrest would probably be his crowning effort. Then would come their promotions and raises. Then later, a book would be written or ghosted, and when it came to her part, a psychiatrist would insert a chapter. She smiled to herself and again tried to feel threatened, but somehow her strange calm held. She wondered what he would say if he knew her life was also threatened, and that only she could take care of it.

CHAPTER 22

Anthony and John, meeting for dinner were planning for the future, trying to salvage the remnants of their father's now almost vanished domains. Had they known more about things, it would have been easier but their ignorance, the government's pouncing, and the remaining members' vigilance in keeping them out of everything rendered them helpless.

This state of things was discussed as well as commiserating the fate of their fathers, as no jury had been vulnerable, nor had any judge now sitting been able to be bribed. They had tacitly agreed that their only source of income rested with the "sideline" which Anthony had always shepherded.

"I tell you, John," Anthony was saying, having decided to bring everything in the open in spite of the humiliation, "I've got to get my own back with her! She practically castrated me. And she had me on the floor -- gun at my mouth!"

"You mean that woman I saw in the gallery posing by that picture?"

"The very same."

"Impossible!"

"And I hadn't even touched her!"

"I thought you were going to fix her for good!"

"I had that in mind, more or less, but I was talking her into doing the job on Silva, then I was going to do the job on her later -- but she didn't give me time -- but I'm going to smear her if it's the last thing I do -- I swear!"

"What are you waiting for?"

"Look John, it's not so easy to tail and shoot in the city. Easier said than done."

"Never seemed to stop our dads -- pardon!" John erased a smile at Anthony's frown.

"And besides, she hardly goes out -- just up there playing the piano, I guess. God knows what the rest are doing. I never saw the artist fellow when I was there, but he's up there all right. That other one goes to the museum every morning, but he doesn't count."

"Well, for Christ sake we've got to do the hit before the people want their money back. The heat's off on him says the grapevine."

"I figured that by that spiel at the museum the night that big announcement he gave."

"Well now I want to take care of her first."

"Look, you've got to find a subtle way to get to her -- all you seem to have in mind is that head-on technique -- old hat."

"And what's your suggestion?"

"You don't have the right bait."

"Bait?"

"O.K. Listen! The dame's high fashion -- right? Plays piano, right? One way or another in one of those areas you can get to her."

"I hear you."

"Leave it to me. I'll see you in a couple of days. Meanwhile just sit tight!"

"O.K." Anthony agreed, glad to leave his headache with John who had been known to have occasional brilliant flashes.

The invitation came several days later delivered in person by the concierge. It carried the seal of one of the famous Parisian fashion houses she had often patronized. Briefly it spoke of the fact that although the master never used his private New York residence for such purposes, for once he was allowing a few favored customers to preview a limited selection of his fall creations at his Southampton home.

Gail Blake realized that she had inherited Miss Bennett's interest in clothes. She decided to attend.

The long graveled walk to the house through the well-kept grounds was pleasant. The house itself looked as if it certainly could belong to the master, so right did it seem standing foursquare looking like a mini-chateau with its turrets and crenellations gleaming in the sunshine. She concluded that she must be quite early as there was not evidence of other guests.

Today belonged to her, and deliberately discarding the suspicion that a car had followed hers on the way out from Manhattan, she decided to be carefree if possible, even frivolous -- perhaps buy a few numbers. She arrived at the door and rang the bell.

A man in a business suit answered. She had expected no less than a butler with all the external elegance.

"I'm here for the showing," she told him.

John looked at her close range with real curiosity, and in spite of himself found her impressive.

"Yes, Madame, right this way," he replied with a slight bow. He led her down a carpeted middle hall and opened a door to the right. The room was empty and she turned questionably to him. He was retiring and closing the door behind him.

She surveyed the obviously professionally decorated room which did not seem to have been set up for any sort of fashion show. However, she took a seat on the ample tufted divan to await developments.

The door opened, and her heart sank as she recognized Anthony. She hated herself for falling into what at hindsight was such an obvious trap. God only knew what he had planned.

As a matter of fact, Anthony had spent a lot of time planning. Mary possibilities had crossed his mind in his search for an adequate revenge before the ultimate kill, among them boiling in oil had figured. He realized he had to forego some because of consideration for the borrowed premises. Behind him came two heavily set muscle bound men known among some as goons. The door shut behind them and for a second there was silence. She moved to open her purse.

"No you don't, you hellion!" Anthony shouted as his men sprang forward. She muttered her teacher's name as she quickly gave each a violent groin kick with Anthony anxiously looking on from a safe distance. It was, however, useless as there was no way with the limited space and two men could she avoid the inevitable. After a ten-minute interval wherein she surprised them with a technique they had not yet studied, they maneuvered her in a wrestling hold and held her while Anthony drew up a chair.

Her skirt was now torn in several places, her jacket ripped and her bag long since knocked to the floor spilling out its contents.

She had not removed her twenty-two since her trip to Anthony's house, and it had spilled to the floor with her cosmetics. She tried to break the hold they had her in to retrieve it, but Anthony reached it first. In any case it would have been a wasted effort. The two men roughly settled her in the chair and in five minutes she was bound with strong thin nylon rope which cut mercilessly into her back- crossed arms and wrists.

The men complained to Anthony that they had not been warned of her capabilities. One had a rapidly swelling eye, the other was coughing from a head butt to his throat. They backed away breathing hard from the struggle. It was clear that she was not going to go quietly.

As they shuffled grumbling from the room, Anthony now moved forward. "You smart ass hinkty bitch!" he growled, looking down at her. "You thought you could get away with what you did to me? Well you've got another thought coming! You bitch!"

She remained silent, overwhelmed with self-recrimination for her stupidity in walking into this trap. But she withheld the satisfaction of conversation which was clearly what he wanted.

He came nearer and slapped her hard. "You hear me talking to you. Answer me!"

She remained silent. He slapped her again. "Before I'm through with you, you'll be glad to talk -- to beg me -- to plead for mercy! You hinkty bitch!"

"What does 'hinkty' mean?" she asked, assuming innocence.

He flushed with rage. "Never mind, bitch. You'll find out! You're going to crawl to me and repeat it a million times! You're going to beg my pardon another million times too."

He sat on the divan and examined her gun. "Even got a fancy gun! Pretty jet set, Miss Bitch! You know what? You're going to get it with your own gun!" He gave a slow smile, coming closer to check her hands and wrists. Resuming his seat, he tossed the gun playfully in the air.

"But first I'm going to make a little lace around your arms and shoulders. No more piano for you -- no more nothing!"

"Anything," she corrected.

"Oh, shut up. In a minute you won't be so fresh!"

John came in at this point. Anthony frowned. He preferred to savor his long fantasized position alone.

"Need any help?" John glanced from one to the other.

"No. This is my job. I told you I could take care of it."

"Oh, so now we're independent, are we? Well, I'd advise you not to dally too long. I see there's been some car hanging around outside. Made some circles around -- maybe it's O.K. But can't be too careful, I say."

Anthony's frown increased as he saw his rehearsed dream being rushed. "Go take a walk, John. You're chicken. Gin Lane has plenty of action. Lots of sightseers come around -- the house is a copy of a French chateau -- visible from the street."

John left slamming the door. Anthony stretched his legs, made himself more comfortable on the couch and smiled unpleasantly.

Her thoughts were reviewing the time she was seated comfortably in the Museum of Modern Art looking at a rare revival of old movies and laughing at the adventures of Pearl White. Now she was the real Pearl White, not the reel one. It was galling to be at the mercy of such a nut -- an incipient sadist whom she had two opportunities to liquidate.

"You see, there are two ways you can get it," he continued, remembering words he had overheard as a kid years ago from the head of the steps as his father spoke softly into the telephone.

"You can cop it the easy way, or you can decide on the hard way -- or if you beg nicely enough, maybe something better will turn up. Look at me! I'm giving you a choice. It depends all on how you behave -- get it?"

"Unhand me, villain," she answered still thinking of the old movie.

He did not recognize the irony, but rose to bend her head back and give her another hard slap. "Don't get smart with me, bitch!" He felt a shade disappointed. She was not reacting as he had imagined when he was visualizing the scene. Even now her face stayed wooden and she showed no signs of any sort of capitulation. He resumed his seat, and decided on the unfailing treatment. He would start now with the gun.

"Look here, Miss Uppity. I've got your gun here -- watch me, since you're the iron lady, maybe this will change your mind." He rose and angled down toward her shoulder, then, changing his mind he decided to work first on her arms tied behind her. He flushed with anger and surprise at the kick on the shins she was able to aim as he passed.

He went to the door and called out. In a moment, the two aides came in with more rope and began tying her legs to the rounds of the chair. This they did silently and efficiently, but with great care not to give her any leeway before they marched out again. "Now for the fun," Anthony said taking a position behind her. He fired once, aiming at one arm and then again at the other, passing around to face her.

She braced for the delayed reaction of the expected pain. The second show made her thoughts skip to Benton and his opportunities to enter her house in Mexico. There was no pain, which told her he had changed her ammunition to blanks.

Quickly she threw her head back to simulate pain and thanked her stars for Benton's meddling.

"That's the only language you understand, Miss hinkty bitch!" he said, now more pleased at her reaction. "Wait till I begin on your shoulders. I'm patient. We don't want to rush this, do we?"

She kept her head back and eyes closed. In this position, numbed by the cutting ropes, overwhelmed by anger at herself and frustration at her helplessness, she achieved a state of semi-consciousness.

Anthony's satisfaction was flawed as a lack of blood told him something was wrong. He looked at the little gun, broke it open and checked the cartridges that were left.

"Damn!" he exploded. "What the hell?" He left the room to get more adequate weapons which included more than a loaded gun.

So complete was her surrender to the semiconscious state she had induced, that she barely heard the commotion outside the door a few minutes later. At this point she really did not care any more, for a vast opening of darkness had yawned and she was gradually falling into it.

Slowly she awakened to become aware of a familiar room which resembled her own bedroom. There were the vertical blinds, the curtains billowing in the small breeze as she slept without air conditioning. The same bone-colored furniture. All accounted for. Why was she covered with this down comforter? Now there came the discomfort of the places the ropes had bitten into her arms and ankles, yet she had the feeling of dreaming and wondered if she was indulging in wishful thinking as she looked around at familiar surroundings.

She still felt at a great disadvantage as the memory of the recent predicament slowly returned. Then came the remembrance of Anthony's rage at finding her twenty-two contained blanks, followed by his leaving the room -- or had he? Suddenly she irrationally pushed everything aside to check her fingernails. Bad luck!

One was chipped -- possibly in the initial struggle with the two men. This, oddly enough triggered anger. She tried to sit up as the scene began to unroll before her as in a moving picture, but sitting up proved difficult.

"Careful! Little by little, Señora," came the voice of Pelayo. He had been sitting unseen by her across the room, but now approached the bed.

Ignoring her aching muscles, she achieved the sitting position. 'I'm here?" she asked. Then, "I'm really here!"

"That is right. You are here," he answered, covering her shoulders with the comforter she had thrown off.

"What happened after -- after..." she hesitated as the impact of the entire situation now bore in on her fully awakened consciousness. Then she became wary. Neither Pelayo or Silva were ever to know.

"You fainted. Yes, you fainted at a friend's house. After you fell, of course."

"After I fell?"

"Maybe before you fell -- but nice you don't remember that unpleasantness. Yes, you fell down a few steps and lost consciousness, it seems. Mr. Benton and a friend brought you here."

"Benton!"

"Yes. It seems he was nearby where you had visited a friend. Frankly, Señora, I do not know the fine details, but he was in such a hurry to get you here and in bed. We had a doctor in..."

"Oh, God -- a doctor..."

"Of course. He brought you around to a real slumber and left. Then..."

"Stop yattering at her and give her more medicine," Silva demanded as he came in with a bottle of cognac on a tray.

"Then Benton had to leave. He said he would return," continued Pelayo.

"That's what I was afraid of," she murmured as Silva, wearing a small apron in which he looked ridiculous, forced a small glass into her hand. In spite of her confusion she realized that Silva was doing "theatre" in affecting the apron. To keep peace she drank the cognac and leaned back to collect her thoughts. Looking down at herself she realized she was wearing one of her nightgowns. She was alarmed.

"Who undressed me?" she demanded looking from one to the other.

"Well, somebody had to do it," Pelayo ventured, "so it fell to me. It was an emergency, Señora. I apologize."

She subsided, realizing that it was the least of the three evils possible. Just so it was not Benton.

Silva drew up a chair and, armed with a second glass poured himself a cognac. "You see, Gail, or Mrs. Duran, or whoever, I keep telling you -- you just don't take your food seriously enough. That fall you had was weakness, undernourishment. I keep telling you that. In this hemisphere..."

"Maestro, spare me -- I'm really not ready for that lecture." She closed her eyes languidly hoping to shut him up.

"What time is it?" she asked.

"About eight hours," Pelayo answered. "Maybe you would like a little dinner -- it's almost time."

"Yes, but nothing too heavy," Silva replied taking charge. "A little consommé, a little breast of boiled chicken, and a small portion of potatoes -- mashed, not much seasoning. Go call down and order it, Pelayo. I'm busy here. Someone's got to watch her. And also a flan. Then maybe a cappuccino."

They'll kill me with kindness, she thought, but it warmed her to see their solicitude. She relaxed and assumed the face of an invalid to please them while a strong wave of thankfulness washed over her. She firmly pushed back the thought of Benton's return.

Silva straightened the comforter and sat again. She stirred and opened her eyes. "And could I have champagne with my dinner?"

"Of course -- nothing like a good wine for the digestion. We will all have some. We will eat in here." He looked around and spotted a round table which he began to prepare.

"All will be ready when they deliver. Just keep resting. You will recover. I will see to that."

As she obeyed, questions came flooding. What had really happened? How had she escaped not only from Anthony, but from the house itself? She had noticed a car which might or might not have been following her, but she couldn't be sure. Then what about her own car? The frustrating part was that she couldn't communicate anything with the two men now determined to pamper her. Obviously Benton had told them some fiction which she, of course, would maintain. Then she suddenly knew that she never, never wanted these two men -- her charges -- to know the whole truth about her. She always wanted them to see her as they now did -- but always.

As she reflected during the dinner that followed, she wondered how it all seemed so normal. There was Pelayo bringing in the covered dishes and following Silva's directions as to placement. Silva, still in his apron, propped up a tray in front of her and proceeded to arrange her plate according to the way he would paint a still life. The champagne was opened and served, and allowing for the cognac already taken, the meal assumed a merry quality which made her sore muscles ache even more as she joined in their laughter. Starting without appetite, she recouped as she went along, ending up even tasting from their plates.

They finally cleared away and again, the picture of Silva piling up dishes and declaring he had often done so in his youth initiated a spate of nervous giggles, especially so since Pelayo, still in his correct pince-nez, was acting as scullery maid, doing the scraping before Silva piled them.

Human frailty took over, however, and within half an hour after dinner she fell into a sound sleep in which none of the day's happenings figured.

More tranquility came with morning. She threw back the coverings everyone had insisted on, and thought stiff and limping, she drew her bath, changed into a long sleeved nightgown to hide the red marks on her arms and returned to bed after filing her chipped nail and carefully making up. Through the long window giving to her part of the terrace, she noted the day was another excellent one. Life was going on as if nothing had happened to her. Yet, there hovered that unsettling interview which she knew there was now no avoiding. It all came back to Benton. Somehow he had saved her, rescued her, and she was now beholden -- very much so. Yet there remained the glaring fact that her nemesis could not longer be postponed. He had saved her for the hangman? The Chair? For the fatal injection?

For shooting at sunrise? It all spelled doom. And just when she had awakened from what amounted to a long coma. Three years of coma -- sleep -- non-living. The paying for what she had done during the time, no matter the motivation, must be expiated. The debt would be collected by Benton.

Oddly enough hunger intervened through the serious thinking; she called for Pelayo.

"Where's my breakfast?" she asked, having decided that since they were going to make her an invalid, she could at least act the part.

"Oh, it's ready -- just what you usually eat. I would not disturb you until you awakened, Señora. You needed that sleep more than ever."

"And Pelayo, I want it with champagne." If she was going to her doom that day, she would jolly well march toward it festooned in a glorious haze. Bring on Benton! She inwardly shouted.

She ate her lamb chop over toast and drank the wine with gusto. Silva came in and nodded approvingly. Pelayo cleared away after leaving her with one of her bedside books. Then the telephone rang, and with a sinking feeling she answered. Of course it was Benton, and without prelude, he announced that he would be over within the hour. As she hung up, she fortified herself with the last bit from the bottle.

An hour later he strode in with much of the same aspect she remembered when he had asked her to join his amateur group -- how long ago had it been? Eons? His heavy chestnut hair was now brushed severely back, the freshly shaved face still redolent of the Paris lotion, the beige summer suit blending with the tan acquired in Mexico.

"You're looking pretty good this morning, considering," he commented after low-keyed greetings. He pulled a chair beside the bed.

As though we only had a strenuous outing in a sailboat the day before, she thought.

"It won't take me long to snap back," she replied.

"Doesn't seem like too much damage done," he continued in the same vein.

"Just some sore muscles, and these darn red lines where the ropes cut. I'm going on my exercise apparatus and get rid of the aches. Oh yes, I chipped a nail when I took on the two musclemen." Her attempt at levity was successful, if his smile was an indication.

"Oh, no! Your nail was <u>chipped</u>? You don't say!"

She felt more comfortable with some of the ice broken, but still tense, she asked, "Could you tell me exactly what happened -- how you knew where I was -- about Anthony -- and where is he, by the way?"

"It's quite a long story..." he began.

"But first -- first off I should thank you for helping me out -- well for saving my life, really. I guess you know he had in mind to chop me up or shoot me up in little pieces."

"Did he indeed?"

"Yes. You see, he was up here and I knocked him about a bit -- he's soft and out of training. I let him go because I didn't want my home desecrated."

"Really?"

"Then when they lured me out to Southampton for the fake fashion show, it was to kill me -- that's certain. But slowly. I have never felt so angry with myself -- so furious with him -- and of course I was scared too..." It was a relief to be able to talk about

228

it, even to Benton whom she knew would turn it all against her in the long run. "I tried to hypnotize myself into a state where I could suspend feeling -- tried to will myself into suspended animation or something."

"When we got to you, that was the case -- you were out of it.'"

"Helped along by that numb feeling in my arms and legs."

"Yes, I suppose."

She noticed his reticence, and suddenly knew that he was not going to tell her very much. He sat there, the perfect protagonist for some discerning director to say lights, camera, action. Maddening how well groomed and unflappable he was, withholding information about life and death -- her life and death, perhaps.

"There's really not much to tell," he said, aware of her natural curiosity. "I knew you were determined to play the lone ranger, so I had you followed -- at first inefficiently, then efficiently. With car telephones it didn't take long for me to locate you. The only risk was would it be soon enough -- to stop you from acting, or them from acting on you. We were in the dark thanks to you. But I had the indications. It's just that you could have made things so much simpler for us."

She turned away and watched the sun on the terrace during an uncomfortable silence. "And Anthony Scavoni?"

"I guess you know about his father's conviction. And as far as Anthony is concerned, I can only tell you he will never be a threat again. To anyone."

"Never?"

"Never."

"I suppose you wouldn't care to go into detail?"

"No, I wouldn't."

The pause told her that a period had been placed on the episode.

"I guess you'd like me to tell you I tied him to a chair and tortured him, right?" he smiled. As she remained silent, he reached in his pocket and handed her the sapphire gun.

"Something you forgot, no doubt," he said. "Shall I just put it in this drawer of the night table? And you car's in your garage downstairs."

She waited, after murmuring an embarrassed thanks. Now he would turn to the heart of the matter. What did he plan for her? How would her new life end and how much time did she have?

"By the way, just what does the word 'tancat' mean? It keeps popping up here and there." He resumed his chair near the bed.

Glad to postpone the inevitable she promptly answered. "It's a Catalan word meaning 'closed'. One sees it all over the shops of Barcelona at lunchtime. It was used to identify the traitor in Silva's group for some reason."

"I see. Well, that's all squared away. Now I'll turn to another matter entirely."

"I know -- in for life!" She gave a hollow laugh. Anything to delay.

"How well you put it," he smiled back. "I'm afraid that's the case."

She reached for her wine glass to find it empty. She had forgotten. Then, unable to meet his eyes, she turned to gaze out at the sun glinting on the terrace. Maybe my last chance, she thought.

"You see, there's been a lot of research recently charting the patterns of love."

Abruptly she turned to him wondering if she had heard correctly or had lost the thread of an earlier conversation. He continued still looking squarely at her.

"There's intimacy, passion and commitment -- the major components. But what usually really brings a couple together recedes as time goes on."

"I don't quite follow you."

"As a matter of fact, people don't know what they can expect when they 'fall in love'," he spoke ironically and smiled. "The quickest to develop, they find, is passion and that's the quickest to fade."

He paused and thought for a moment. She started to speak but he held up his hand for silence and continued. "Strong emotional commitment is really essential to a long-term relationship. You can't take it for granted."

He obviously wanted to finish with a memorized passage, but she remained confused.

"Love is so ephemeral," he now seemed to be more relaxed as his face softened. "You can't count on it. Passion peaks then declines," he paused. "I said all that for a good reason," his voice lowered. "I wanted to warn you how it could be."

"How it could be? What?"

"Because in spite of all that rigmarole I just recited, I want you to know that I know absolutely nothing about love -- I read that in some magazine."

"Oh?"

"The only thing I can tell you is that I must have you -- for life."

In the long silence that followed, he watched as her face changed from bewilderment to incredulity and then to something else he could not identify.

She never realized the time it took to make a decision of a lifetime, and for a lifetime, the components of which had arrived minutes before, for time had lost its meaning. It took on the dimensions of an eternity.

He understood her silence. He himself had only faced up to his incredible feeling when he had been alerted to her imminent danger in the Southampton house. His panic and concern had plainly told him what he was trying to ignore.

Now he waited and watched as she closed her eyes, head back on the pillows. She had to deal with the dazzling light that pervaded her. When she opened them again, he was still there, waiting.

"I wonder if I'm dreaming it all."

"No, you heard correctly. It's probably an unexpected development..."

"An understatement..."

"But I don't know how else to put it. I just said I know nothing about love. I flunked it once. I'm leveling with you -- just want you, one way or another, for life."

"Aren't you supposed to arrest me? Or arrange it?"

He smiled. "I'm glad you mentioned that. I could, you know. And that gives me an unfair advantage which I have no intention of not taking. So let that influence your answer."

As all the pieces slowly began to come together, she wondered if all this time in her fear she had been running from her safe haven, her well being which Gail Blake wanted, but never expected. To have a real life, and with Gregory Benton?

Parrying for time, she spoke. "So it amounts to a veiled threat you're offering?

Prison or you?"

"Oh, no, not veiled at all. It's outright!" Then in another tone he said, "Look, Gail, I know now it's a predestined thing. I should have understood it that night we danced in Mexico."

She almost smiled, but still dazed, she felt as if dreaming a strange dream in a strange land.

He continued. "I'm worried about only two things: First if you'll accept me, and second if it's possible that with all you've been through -- your extreme reaction to tragedy -- you just might have a breakdown -- a critical one."

She now smiled, and he noted it was the first real one he had seen her give. It was the other face Silva had painted. Even her voice seemed different, softer. "I appreciate your concern, but please believe me -- I have no intention of having a breakdown because I have paid my dues. I have suffered the tragedy of my husband -- the unnecessary tragedy of his death, then the rape and murder of my daughter on top of that. The gods did this to me, and it made me different -- crazy if you will. I have already suffered."

"I know that, but didn't know how you analyzed it."

"I can spend the rest of my life free -- as Gail Blake."

"No, as Gail Benton. Still the same initials on the guest towels."

They both began to laugh, a fraction overdone in the relief of the tension.

"I hate it that Clem knew how I felt before I did. He told me I'd better do something about you right now before you got into any more 'fixes'. I really believe he talks western now naturally, he's done it for so long." His smile faded as he looked at her more seriously. "Then I take it that you -- you..."

"Yes," she interrupted. "You can take it that I..." she paused as they both silently recognized what the moment meant.

"Just one thing -- one favor," he sat on the bed and took her hand. "For God's sake, never tell Clem or anybody else I've never even kissed you, much less..."

"Good you mentioned that," she answered still smiling, "because that's my little possibility for blackmail too."

"Then we're 'a mano'? Even?"

"Yes, 'a mano'."

"But don't think I haven't got plans to make up for this puritanical situation. And by the way, you're throwing in your lot with a jobless man. I resigned this morning'"

In a spontaneous gesture she covered his hand with her other, "I'm so glad. It's the icing."

He laughed, "So I couldn't have arrested you. But we'll do fine. I like your attitude. And I'll get something to do."

"No trouble for you to earn a living. You wowed them in Albuquerque or was it Cuernavaca?"

"And don't forget my travel articles! And I've saved a bit' and there's the house in Cuernavaca."

"I'm not the least worried," she spoke calmly, but an overwhelming unexpected happiness flooded her. She was glad when Emily, who had been hovering in the background, now jumped up on the bed, wanting to be a part of whatever she sensed was happening.

A formal tapping on the open bedroom door precluded Silva's entrance followed by Pelayo with a magnum of champagne surrounded by four glasses. He pointed a warning finger at them.

"Not too fast, my friends. I just happened to be passing by, and even if I do not always understand English, I know all about the two of you." He made himself comfortable in a chair and continued. "She came to me out of the purple sunset and before you both walk back into it, let me be the one to arrange things. I am almost finished with my New York period. We will shortly go back to Mexico to my villa where I will chaperon Gail until..."

"Oh great!" Benton interrupted, "That's all we needed -- a chaperon!" They all began to laugh.

"...Until I can arrange a proper wedding in my garden. She'll wear lilac, of course -- under the arbor -- Pelayo, you'd better see to it, and I have a good design in mind for the altar -- all flowers."

Benton and Gail exchanged glances which telegraphed their helplessness.

"I realize my life has not adhered to the bourgeois idea that most people have of everything on earth, but that is not to say that I do not feel responsible for my model and protectress here. Of course I foresaw all this and I want your friend to know he was not the only one to know how things stood between you."

"Oh, of course the bride and groom are always the last to know, right?' Benton asked as he raised her hand to his lips. "But don't anybody worry, we're going to catch up -- fast."

It was too much. Her eyes had filled and she sobbed. He caught her and held her as she buried her head in his shoulder.

"<u>Dios mio</u>, Pelayo, when are you going to serve that champagne?" Silva scolded, "Can't you see we're all waiting for it?"

THE END

Miss Bennett is happy at last!